THE MISTLETOE MISTRESS

THE
MISTLETOE
MISTRESS
A NOVELLA

MADDISON MICHAELS

BOOKS BY MADDISON MICHAELS

The Saints and Scoundrels Series

Novels:

The Devilish Duke

The Elusive Earl

The Sinful Scot

Novellas:

The Mistletoe Mistress

The Bachelor Bounty Series

Coming 2020

** US spelling used throughout**

Edited by Author Designs

Cover design by Maddison Fitzsimmons

Cover photos from Period Images & Getty Images

ISBN: 978-0-6487117-0-4

First Edition December 2019

For my Family
The absolute loves of my life!

CHAPTER 1

LONDON, 1855

Bachelors, boredom and whiskey, were never a particularly good combination, and when mixed with a rather dubious wager made by three of London's most notorious rakes, it was a recipe for disaster in the making.

A fact, Michael Drake, the Viscount Blackthorn, probably should have considered before agreeing to the whole darn thing. Christmas festivities had never been a particularly joyful occasion for him and he'd been especially bored at this ball, so when his two friends, both equally as jaded as Michael himself had suggested the bet he'd agreed.

After all, since returning from the war Michael had held little interest in anything. Perhaps a mistletoe mistress might be just what he needed to rid himself of the listlessness that had plagued him since his return from the Crimea. It might even perhaps stop the nightmares that had been stalking his sleep.

"So, we are in agreement then," Devlin Markham, the Duke of Huntington stated, his deep voice raised to be heard over the string quartet playing from the ballroom. He straightened from where he'd been leaning over the balustrade gazing at the guests below.

The three of them had sought solace from the dancing and gossiping, preferring to escape to one of the alcoves upstairs to enjoy a nice glass of whiskey devoid of interruption while still being able to see what was going on without having to partake in any of the tedium.

"We shall each ante up one thousand pounds," Huntington continued. "And whoever is the first to seduce the very next lady to walk under Lady Pembrook's famed mistletoe, shall be the winner of the wager. Provided of course, the woman is not an innocent." He handed each of them a sprig of mistletoe he'd recently plucked from the plant decoration itself.

"Goodness no! I have no wish to be forced into marriage," George Bainbridge, the Marquis of St. Giles, exclaimed, eyeing the mistletoe in distress. "Neither of you think there's any truth to the legend of Lady Pembrook's mistletoe, do you?"

A grin split Huntington's lips, and Michael couldn't help but smile too as he also took a sprig of the greenery and slipped it in his pocket, completely unconcerned over the legend. It was absolute nonsense to think a plant could determine a man's matrimonial fate.

Which is what they'd all been discussing and had led to the wager. Michael shook his head, thinking not for the first time he probably should have refused rather than agree to it. None of them had any idea who would be the next lady to walk under the archway, and the idea of seducing even an enticing Madonna—not that he expected such a creature to walk through the arbor—was tiring.

That very thought in itself was enough for Michael to realize how much the war had changed him. Especially how Edward's death had. He'd lost his best-friend from childhood that day and nothing had been the same since. Especially as it was Michael who had killed him.

A fact he doubted he would ever be able to forget or forgive.

As usual, his stomach twisted into a knot and he had to swallow back the bitterness and simmering regret that still consumed him.

Probably why he'd agreed to the wager. Anything to distract himself from his guilt would be a good thing, particularly as he no longer had the war, or the suicide missions he'd always volunteered for to divert his attention.

Once he would have relished the idea of winning such a wager, yet now he felt seducing a lady was going to be more of a chore than a pleasure. And for some strange reason the mistletoe nestled in his pocket felt decidedly uncomfortable. Not that he in any way believed any of the nonsense about the stuff.

"My friend," Huntington finally answered St. Giles. "The very idea that Lady Pembrook's mistletoe holds magical matrimonial powers is ludicrous beyond measure, and is part of the reason we shall all keep a sprig of the stuff in our pockets until this wager has a winner. Then when no marriages are forthcoming, we shall have proved that the tales surrounding the stuff are completely false."

"Uh huh." St. Giles did not sound convinced. "Then why worry about the lady being an innocent or not, if you don't believe the tale? What if it does make one fall in love?" Fear lit up the man's eyes with the thought.

For years word had spread that Lady Pembrook's mistletoe held special, almost magical qualities beyond that of normal mistletoe. It was whispered that if a man took a sprig of Lady Pembrook's mistletoe and kept it in his pocket, that the next unattached lady he kissed would be destined to be the love of his life and they would marry. Utter nonsense in Michael's book, but apparently it had happened so often that some couples even carried out the ritual on purpose.

What poor, pathetic fools.

"Love is a wasted emotion," Huntington said, his words completely matter-of-fact. "The two of you know that to be the case. Innocents are the path to matrimony, my friends, which is something I have no intention of partaking in. Ever. Hence why I refuse to have anything to do with virgins. I will not be forced into marriage by anyone."

Michael couldn't imagine anyone forcing the Devil Duke to do anything he didn't want to. The man was formidable in business and with the ladies, and though Michael had a similar reputation, even he drew the line at dallying with innocent virgins. "I couldn't agree with you more," he replied. "Besides, women with experience are infinitely more delightful and willing to be adventurous in the bedchamber." He pushed in closer to the balustrade, as a woman wearing a dark blue gown slowly came into view from the entrance hall, though she was still too far away to see her face.

"It looks like we're about to see who the lucky lady is," St. Giles enthused. "As there's a woman who looks like she's about to cross under the mistletoe archway. I do hope she's attractive."

"All women are attractive, my friend." Huntington grinned. "You just have to look carefully is all. Particularly under the surface."

"Debatable," St. Giles grumbled.

"Well provided she's not a virgin," Michael reminded them, "then regardless of what she looks like, or whether she's married, or a widow, she'll be acceptable for the wager. Are we agreed?"

The two other men nodded, their bodies braced forward and leaning over the balustrade in an effort to see the woman's identity.

As she walked further toward the archway Michael allowed his gaze to follow the sapphire colored material of the woman's gown from her feet up. The dress molded a tiny waist, before gently weaving its way up to cover the creamiest porcelain chest, with just a hint of bosoms showing beneath its satiny exterior. His glance skimmed higher up the woman's graceful neck, across her determined little chin and pert nose, to eyes framed by the thickest of lashes. Lashes he'd seen before.

A cold sweat broke out on his brow and his heart began to thud as he recognized that it was Miss Holly Jenkins he stared at with unabated lust. Good God, it was Edward's sister. What the devil was she doing here? And why the hell was the thrum of desire thick in his blood, simply from peering down at her?

His heart dropped as she walked under the mistletoe archway.

But then dread gave way to relief. Innocents were off limits in this stupid bet of theirs. Thank, bloody, goodness.

"She's an absolute angel," St. Giles exclaimed, rubbing his hands together. "Even from this distance I don't think I've ever seen such green eyes." He glanced over at Huntington and Michael. "And that ebony hair of hers, along with her ample bosom that I could bury my head in—simply delicious. I'm going to enjoy beating the two of you in this wager."

"Damn it! You won't be beating us at anything. She's off limits," Michael growled. "Do you understand me, St. Giles? Off limits."

"Why?" Huntington's tone was completely neutral, but Michael didn't like the look of keen interest in his gaze as the man's eyes stayed locked on Holly. The Devil Duke hadn't earned his moniker for being any sort of saint, and most especially not with the ladies.

"Because that is *Miss* Holly Jenkins," Michael grated out.

"She is unmarried and hence will not play any part in our wager. Are we clear?"

Huntington sighed, devilish anticipation glittering in his dark blue eyes. "My friend, you've been away for too long in the Crimea."

Michael paused, and stared levelly at the man not liking where this was heading. "Explain yourself."

The duke's eyes flared in annoyance at the command, but Michael didn't give a damn. Friend or not, Michael wasn't going to let him anywhere near Miss Jenkins. And if he had to show Huntington physically that he meant business, then show him physically he would.

"She may have been *Miss* Jenkins before you left, but she's now *Mrs*. Carlton." Huntington's eyes narrowed down upon the lady in question, just before she darted off down an adjacent hallway. "She is no virgin and is firmly within the purviews of our wager, my friend."

"She's married?" Michael couldn't comprehend how he wouldn't have known such a thing. True, he had spent the last two years in the Crimea, but surely he would have known if Miss Holly Jenkins had married. He had after all bestowed on her and her two sisters, extremely generous dowries, subsequent to having promised Edward he'd look after them. But none of the dowries had been touched yet.

"Oh, that's excellent news! Married women are always so much easier to seduce. They are so bored with their husbands and are begging for some adventure. Makes them supremely easy pickings," St. Giles enthused, leaning out over the balcony railing as far as he could in an attempt to get another look at her before she completely disappeared from view. "You chaps will have no chance as I daresay she's bound to be more attracted to my blond good looks and robust charm, rather than the two of you with your dark and broody personas." He pulled away from the balcony and turned around to smile at them both. "She won't be able to resist me. That money is as good as mine!"

"Damn it, I said she was off limits!" Michael didn't know what came over him, but he grabbed St. Giles by the lapels of his jacket and spun him toward the wall, pinning him against it. "Married or not!"

"Well she's a widow, actually," Huntington relaxed back against the other wall, merely watching Michael tower over St. Giles his hands still clenched tightly against the man's jacket.

"Widowed?" Now Michael was getting downright confused.

"Yes," Huntington confirmed. "Supposedly her husband died only a few months after their wedding and she's only recently come out of mourning to re-enter society."

"You seem to know an awful lot about her." Michael narrowed his eyes toward his friend not liking the look of contemplation in Huntington's expression.

Huntington shrugged. "I always pay attention. Especially to attractive females. And personally I prefer widows. They're independent and have no wish to relinquish that freedom to another marriage. Your Mrs. Carlton shall be the perfect mistletoe mistress for our wager."

"She's not *my* anything. And she's too good and decent for any of us." Michael emphasized his words by pressing St. Giles more firmly against the wall. And once again he wished he'd never agreed to such a stupid bet in the first place.

"I don't doubt it," Huntington agreed. "But she intrigues me, and you said so yourself, widows are acceptable in our wager."

"Not this one." Michael didn't know why he was feeling so enraged with the thought of his friends trying to seduce the woman. Apart from the fact that he'd promised her brother on his deathbed that he would look after her and her two other sisters. And letting two notorious rakes try to seduce her as part of a bet was not looking after her by any measure. It's why he'd stayed away from her upon his return three months ago. His reputation would only tarnish her own, though he hadn't known she was a widow, so her reputation wasn't as much a concern anymore.

"You care for her then?" Huntington's eyes turned to Michael. There was an intensity in them that Michael didn't like at all. "Because if you do have feelings for her, then of course St. Giles and I will leave her alone."

Michael held Huntington's gaze without blinking. "I do not have feelings for the chit, I'm simply trying to protect her." He was hoping to convince not only Huntington, but himself too. In truth, he'd always been slightly intrigued and attracted to Holly, despite her often berating him in the past. But of course he'd never acted on such feelings, nor would he ever do so. He had every intention to honor the promise he made to his best-friend on his deathbed. Regardless of the lust he still felt for Holly. And lust he could control.

"She's a widow my friend. She doesn't need your protection. Besides, if it's not one of us to seduce her someone else will." He flicked a speck of lint from his midnight black tailored jacket. "She's too attractive to stay unattached for long. Besides, she may be looking for a protector now that she's out of mourning."

The very words turned Michael's thoughts murderous.

"Will you let me go?" St. Giles ground out, pushing against Michael's fists, but Michael didn't budge an inch. "And Huntington's quite correct. The other men of the Ton will be sniffing around her before the night's over."

Huntington straightened from where he was lounging against the balustrade. "Are you certain you don't have any feelings for her then?"

Michael's fists balled up even tighter against St. Giles'

lapels and he had to make a determined effort to loosen them slightly. Of course, he didn't have feelings for Holly Jenk—Carlton. Edward's younger sister had always been extremely bossy, with decided opinions about right and wrong, and she'd very much considered Michael a bad influence over her brother and had always been lambasting them as young men over their escapades. She'd been a bloody pain. An attractive bloody pain, but a pain, nonetheless.

In the end she'd been right though. If it hadn't been for Michael, Edward would still be alive. "Apart from protectiveness and a wish to keep her safe. No. I don't have any feelings for the woman."

Huntington raised his brow in an expression Michael suspected meant he did not believe him. "Then, as she fits the criteria for our wager," Huntington continued, "she's fair game. Now why don't you let poor St. Giles go. You're crinkling up his lapels terribly, and he's already at a disadvantage in securing the lovely Mrs. Carlton's attentions going up against us."

"Bollocks I am," St. Giles ground out as Michael released him, before taking a step backward. "And what was all that about?" He demanded to Michael, brushing down the material of his lapels, a decided expression of annoyance on his normally affable visage. "What's gotten into you?"

Michael drew in a rather long breath. "Damn it. I'm sorry St. Giles." And he was. Though he had no qualms about engaging in a physical confrontation, St. Giles was as close to a friend as he had, and he didn't normally get physical with friends. Not that he really had any friends apart from these two. "I don't know what came over me."

"A woman is what came over you." Huntington laughed. "But thankfully you don't have feelings for her, isn't that so? Otherwise, goodness knows how else you would have reacted. 'Tis lucky for St. Giles and I, that you don't care for her, isn't it?"

There was a definite note of sarcasm in Huntington's voice, but Michael chose to ignore it. "Perhaps we should simply choose another lady for the wager? Then there would be no issue."

"There's no issue now," Huntington was quick to point out. "You said it yourself, you don't have feelings for her. Besides, Mrs. Carlton is ravishing. I find my interest stirred."

"And mine," St. Giles seconded. "In fact, I can't think of a more delightful quarry than the stunning Mrs. Carlton. It will be a pleasure to try to get her in my bed."

"You won't be bedding her," Michael growled, as he took a step toward St. Giles who was only an inch shorter than Michael's own six-foot-two frame.

St. Giles squared his chest in response, his green eyes staring accusingly at Michael's blue ones. "What has gotten into you! You've never had such issues before regarding our wagers and the women involved. Yet now you're getting physical with me over a woman you supposedly don't even care about."

"Would the two of you both relax." Huntington stepped between the two men, pushing them both apart. "She's a widow and can make her own choices." He was pointedly looking at Michael. "If you don't want either of us to bed her, Michael, then you be the one to win the wager."

"Damn it then I will!" The words rushed out of Michael's mouth before he could think better of them.

"Good," Huntington said. "May the best man win." And with a curt nod, he turned on his heel and retreated down the back stairs to brave the throng below.

St. Giles simply stared at Michael for a moment, before shaking his head and following the duke.

Michael exhaled harshly as his friends left, before turning

back to the balcony and casting his eyes down across the guests. Bloody hell. What had he just agreed to? He wasn't going to sleep with Edward's sister, even if she was a widow and made every cell of his body scream to possess her. She was from a good family and he would make damn sure those two libertines didn't get so much as even a sniff of her. Which meant he would have to stick closely to her.

He would protect her from them, and even from himself, if he had to.

Now all he had to do was find her, before those two idiot friends of his. He'd seen her hurry down the hall toward Lord Pembrook's study. Which in itself did beg the question of not only what Holly was doing attending the rather notorious ball in the first place, but what was she doing heading off down a corridor, away from the festivities?

CHAPTER 2

THEY SAID darkness was a thief's friend. They lied.

All it did was make Holly's job of picking the lock to Lord Pembrook's safe a great deal more difficult than it normally would be. Blast it! She had to get it open, and soon too, before her absence was noted.

A whisper of awareness danced along her skin as a slight draft reached the nape of her neck.

She spun her head around and glanced over her shoulder, certain she'd heard something but there was nothing but the great hulking darkness of Lord Pembrook's study. Just shadows and dust.

Odd, but she could have sworn she'd felt someone's presence. "Oh Holly, stop being a ninny and get on with it," she whispered, hoping that the words would reassure her.

But a niggle of awareness still lingered and try as she might, she couldn't dismiss the feeling she wasn't alone. Clearly she was more on edge than usual with this clandestine activity. Shaking her head, she returned her attention back onto the sole purpose of her visit this evening; getting the safe open, and quickly.

Perhaps she should light a lamp? If she did, she'd have the thing open in less than thirty seconds; instead she'd been standing in the dark for over two minutes trying to coax it open. Time, she did not have, not if she didn't want to be discovered.

"Come on my sweet," she crooned to the lock as she leaned forward and began to once again manipulate her lock picks inside the lock barrel from pure touch alone. "Open up for me. There's a good thing." Her sisters often teased her for talking to the locks as she picked them, but invariably it always seemed to work. And a few moments later the pins in the tumbler slowly clicked into place and she twisted the lock to triumphantly open the safe's door. Thank goodness!

She reached inside with her gloved hand but felt nothing but a small empty square of space inside the bottom of the safe.

"No, no, no! This can't be!" There couldn't be nothing in there. "Darn it all to hell!" Holly knew she shouldn't swear and that blasphemy was a sin, but some situations simply warranted a more expressive use of the English language. And this was definitely one such occasion.

How could the safe be empty? The letters were meant to be inside.

Heedless of the possibility of being caught, Holly twisted around to the desk behind her; a great big piece of walnut oak dominating a large portion of the room and which she'd already checked didn't contain Lady Clare's stolen letters, but it did have a lamp sitting on its surface. A lamp she would have to risk lighting to confirm that nothing was in the safe. She had to be sure, her very friend's reputation was at risk.

She felt around briefly for the box of matches next to the lamp and then took one out and struck it against the tin.

A flicker of light flared from the match and she wasted no time in lighting the lamp.

Warmth flooded the room, and the light eased her nerves even though it could spell trouble if someone saw the illumination shining from under the door. "Time to make certain nothing is in there." She took the lamp in her hands and turned back to the safe.

"I'd forgotten you often talk to yourself," a deeply masculine voice drawled from the depths of the darkness. "Though I do remember you used to enjoy picking locks as a hobby. I had no idea you'd graduated to doing so for monetary gain. How interesting."

Holly stifled a scream as she spun around to the blackness, holding the light in front of her like a weapon. Her pulse was galloping like wildfire and goosebumps crawled along her skin. "Show yourself, sir! Whoever you are."

A shadow moved only a few feet from her and Holly nearly dropped the lamp. All her senses seemed to heighten as the man unfurled himself from where he'd been leaning against the wall in a dark spot of the room next to a bookcase to her left. *"Lord Blackthorn?"*

Were her eyes deceiving her? Or was one of the most notorious rake-hells of the Ton, a man she'd regularly locked horns with as a child for corrupting her brother, even though she was nearly four years younger than the both of them, standing there in front of her with a curious expression on his wickedly handsome face.

"Is that really you?" She blinked and had to resist bolting for the door. Michael would never harm her, that she knew for certain, but after all the years she'd chastised him for being up to no good she really didn't fancy explaining her actions. Though she could tell from the look in those ridiculously blue eyes of his, that he wasn't going to let her go without an explanation. "Oh damn it, it is you isn't it!"

"You swear a lot more than I remember too." His voice was like warm honey as it washed over her, and Holly had to concentrate on what he was actually saying. No wonder the man was so accomplished with the ladies.

Holly had never been taken in by the smoothly accomplished rakes of the ton, but Michael had always been another story, even though she had tried to convince herself over the years that he was an out and out bounder, a part of her had always been a tiny bit affected by him.

Alright, if she was being truthful with herself, a lot affected. And she was completely unimpressed with herself for feeling that way. The fact that she was now six-and-twenty and his very presence was still enough to send a shiver down her spine, was completely humiliating. She'd thought she was too sensible and older now to be taken in by his charm. But she'd forgotten just how very charismatic the man was, and how a part of her had always been drawn to him as much as she'd fought against it. And he had no idea. Which was definitely a blessing as she'd be mortified if he knew how he affected her.

Absolutely mortified.

"What are you doing here?" she demanded, slamming down the lamp and placing her hands on her hips. "You scared the living daylights out of me, sneaking in here and skulking in the shadows, not saying anything for the longest time!"

The man straightened his tall frame and took a step forward into the light. His cobalt blue eyes shone fiercely with a seemingly amused expression. Clearly, he was having fun at her discomfort. The cad.

"Well?" She began to tap her foot against the wooden floor boards. "I'm waiting for a response, my lord."

"You're certainly still as bossy as ever, aren't you?" He grinned, taking another step toward her, his eyes never leaving her own. "But please stop with the 'my lord' nonsense. You used to call me Michael and I see no reason not to continue doing so now. In fact, I always rather enjoyed our discussions when we were younger. You had such a way of saying my name with just the right amount of exasperation and displeasure, that I entirely looked forward to making you say it. Vexing you was one of my guilty pleasures."

"Well I certainly did call you Michael when I was vexed with you! However, that was when we were younger, and it would be entirely inappropriate to call you so now," she replied, unable to stop the gulp that rose in her throat as she tilted her head up to his, refusing to be the first to break eye contact. She'd forgotten just how tall and broad of shoulders he actually was, and how petite she felt in comparison, which was silly as she wasn't considered short by any measure. Average perhaps, but not short. Though her five-foot-six-inch frame definitely felt short when standing next to him. But he still hadn't answered her question. "I see that you are still a master at deflecting questions."

He laughed, and the rich melodic sound filled the room.

She reached forward and grabbed his arm. "Hush, or else we shall be discovered in here." The touch of her fingers against the material of his jacket sent a jolt of heat all the way up her arm to the very core of her being. Involuntarily, she flinched and quickly dropped her hand away, taking a hasty step backward.

Space. She needed to put some space between them so she could think clearly.

"If we are discovered I shall simply say I'm in here seducing you," Michael said, sounding entirely too comfortable with the excuse.

He winked at her and she went weak at the knees. *Silly*

knees. "You wouldn't dare say such a thing. My reputation would be ruined if you did."

"But you are a widow now aren't you?" he asked, almost with a look of disappointment in the cobalt of his gaze. "Surely being found in my company would only enhance your appeal?"

Guilt plunged low in the depth of her stomach. "You heard I was a widow?"

Michael nodded. "Just this evening. I had no idea you'd even married, to be honest." He paused for a moment, appearing at a sudden loss for words. "I'm...I'm sorry for your loss, Holly. If I had known sooner, I would have conveyed my condolences before this evening." He dragged a hand through his hair. "Even that sounds rather empty saying it aloud. I should have been there for you and I wasn't, and for that I am sorry."

"It's fine," Holly rushed out. "I mean; why would you be there for me? We haven't seen each other in years. Not since Edward's funeral. In fact, I didn't really ever expect to see you again."

"No of course you didn't. Why would you? I always let everyone down, at least according to my father." He took a step back from her and then smiled, though there was little humor in his gaze. "You know, your husband never requested your dowry."

"He didn't?" She hoped her voice sounded calm because inside her heart was racing about a million miles an hour. "He was a very proud man, my husband." At least she imagined he was, it was hard to keep track of what one's fictional dead husband was or was not. "Perhaps he didn't wish to take any money from someone of your, um, station?"

An indecipherable shadow crossed his handsome face. "You mean from someone with my tarnished reputation, don't you?"

Holly pursed her lips. "Actually, no. I meant because he was only a mister and didn't particularly want to have anything to do with aristocracy. I doubt Harold had any notion of your rather, um, infamous reputation with the ladies and such…"

"Harold? You married a man named Harold?"

She gasped. "Don't you dare insult his name, Michael Drake!"

She'd spent hours deciding on Harold's name, thinking it rather noble, particularly for someone she'd always intended to kill off soon after inventing him. "Harold was a paragon of a man. Always attentive and kind. So sweet and generous. Why, he was always reading me poetry and bringing me flowers. Attending upon me all the time, ensuring my needs were well and truly met. He was the most wonderful husband a girl could ever imagine having." And he had been. Harold had been perfect in her imagination. In that, she was not lying at all.

Michael raised a brow. "Forgive me for insulting him. That was particularly crass of me."

"It was," Holly agreed, a twinge of guilt once again flittering across her awareness. Though it was crass of him, particularly if Harold had been real. But Michael didn't know Holly had invented him. Only her two sisters knew. And that's how it would stay. How it had to stay. If people realized she'd invented a husband, even if it had been to protect herself and her sisters, she'd never be able to show her face at social events again. Which would mean the loss of her secret income. "In any event, you still haven't answered my question of what you're doing here sneaking into this room and scaring me half to death!"

"I promise I shall say nothing about your rather nefarious activities surrounding the safe. Cross my heart." This time a grin accompanied another wink, which certainly didn't help strengthen her knees. The man's smile had always been dangerous to any woman in the vicinity.

"Can you be serious for one moment." She tried to sound stern, but she feared that her voice was sounding rather breathless.

"Very well," he replied, his face turning serious. "In truth, I'm here because of you."

"You are?" How had he even known she was in here? She hadn't seen him and had been careful to make sure she hadn't been observed entering Pembrook's study; at least, she thought she had.

"Yes," he said. "I saw you slipping away down here and came to find you. I suspected you might be up to something, although I've got to admit that it didn't cross my mind that you'd be robbing a safe." He shrugged, like it mattered little to him if she did so or not. "It probably should have considering your interest in locks."

"Oh, for goodness sakes! I'm not robbing anything."

"Of course, you're not." His glance swiveled between herself and the now open safe, disbelief written all over his face. "Simply practicing your lock picking skills instead of dancing, are you?"

Holly crossed her arms in front of her chest. "You can cease with the sarcasm, thank you very much. I'm actually trying to retrieve something that was already stolen. Something that does not belong to Lord Pembrook."

"Having no luck finding it either, I take it?"

A large sigh left her lips. "None whatsoever I'm afraid. And now that you've shown up, things are even more complicated."

"They are?"

"Of course, they are!" she cried, picking up the lamp and swiveling back toward the safe. "You are certain to try to make me explain what's going on here."

"You always were a smart girl."

Holly was positive she could detect amusement in his tone, but underneath she could also hear the absolute certainty in his voice. Michael had always been like a dog with a bone and never let anything go, always having to know exactly what was going on. Rather frustrating, even if it did remind her of herself, which meant he wouldn't be satisfied with any lie. She knew that from experience. "Oh, very well. I shall explain the situation to you, but not here. We can't be caught anywhere near here." She quietly shut the door to the safe and pulled out her pins from the lock. The tumblers clicked back into place, once again locking the mechanism.

Michael leaned over her shoulder, peering at the lock. "You didn't leave a scratch," he murmured in her ear. "Very impressive."

Holly tried very hard to ignore the shiver of wicked delight that coursed down her spine as his breath caressed her neck. Good lord, the man's pull was dangerous. She turned around to face him only to find herself within inches of him. Her lips were suddenly dry as the smell of sandalwood and whiskey filled her nostrils, intoxicating in its heady scent.

Concentrate, Holly, concentrate.

He was only a man and certainly not the sort to lose one's calm in front of. No. If he knew he was affecting her so, he'd use the knowledge to his advantage. She raised her chin and returned her attention back to his comment. "Of course, I left no scratches. I'm a professional. But how do you even know that lock picking could potentially leave scratches?"

Was she imagining it, or did Michael just inch closer to her? Holly was sure she could feel the heat radiating from his chest mere inches away from her own.

"Let's just say that the positions I was placed in during the war taught me a lot of things."

"They did?" Oh goodness, his lips were so close to her own. His full and deliciously sensual lips, that she was sure could kiss a woman senseless.

"Yes. I was always the one stupid enough to volunteer for the dangerous missions that inevitably placed me in rather sticky situations. I learned some very useful things," he replied, his voice a husky whisper in the silent room.

His head lowered closer to her own, and for a mad moment Holly wanted nothing more than to know what his lips felt like against hers. What it felt like to be kissed senseless, just as in the novels her sisters devoured, and how Holly had once secretly imagined it would feel to have Michael kiss her. How he'd probably kissed many women senseless over the years.

The thought was sobering. What on earth was she thinking?

She reached up to push him away, but then the door to the study suddenly flew open, a man holding a lamp was silhouetted in the doorway. They'd been discovered! Could this night get any worse?

CHAPTER 3

BEFORE HOLLY COULD BLINK, Michael's lips descended onto her own, his hands reaching around her waist and pulling her in tightly against him. His mouth plundered hers; a delicious onslaught that was over even before it really began, when he wrenched his mouth away and turned toward the now opened doorway.

"I say, what are you two doing in my study?" The pinched voice from the door sounded highly perturbed.

Holly felt her heart drop. It was Lord Pembrook. If he saw her here, he would know exactly what she was up to. Which would not bode well for her friend.

"Sorry, old chap," Michael yelled. "I was just trying to sneak in some private time alone with my friend."

"Is that you, Blackthorn?" Pembrook asked, relief in his voice.

"It is indeed," Michael replied, his body still protecting Holly from Pembrook's view. "Apologies for using your study, Pembrook. And if you'll give me but a moment to become presentable, if you know what I mean, we shall return to the ball."

Pembrook tried to peer further into the darkness, in what Holly was certain was an attempt to see who Michael was shielding, but thankfully Michael's broad chest was doing a thorough job of hiding her from the man's view.

"Of course, of course." Pembrook chortled. "Take your time." And with a wink, the man closed the door, his footsteps echoing away as he retreated down the hall.

Michael swirled back around to face her. "Well that was close."

Holly shuddered. "That was terrifying."

"The kiss or Pembrook?" Michael asked. "And I do hope the answer is Pembrook." There was amusement again in his voice.

Holly swatted him on the arm. "This is no time for jokes. Of course, I'm talking about Pembrook. If he'd seen me, he would have suspected what I was up to and then things would have gotten nasty."

"Well I'm glad it wasn't the kiss," Michael replied. "Though it certainly wasn't my best, rushed as it was. I shall be happy to promptly remedy that impression though."

"Are you ever serious?" Holly took a step around him and headed for the door.

Michael reached his arm out to grab her own, gently pulling her to a stop. "Who says I wasn't being serious?"

Holly pulled back her arm to swat him again, only this time, he pulled her in close and his lips captured her own. But instead of the hastiness of their previous kiss, with this one he took his time as his lips gently teased her own apart, pressing softly but firmly against her. Without warning, her anger at him diminished only to be replaced by a growing need. A hunger to taste and touch him as she'd never felt before.

A sense of wonder and longing engulfed her. His lips were pillow soft but oh so delicious, and then when his tongue touched hers, softly coaxing a response, Holly couldn't help but moan.

Good Lord, the sensations of pleasure were consuming her as a deep aching desire radiated from her core. She pushed her body against his, reveling at the feel of his broad chest against her bosoms. The man was a sin. A deliciously sensual sin that she was suddenly craving. She couldn't get enough of him and the urge to be closer to him, wound its way through her.

She'd felt so alone for so long. Of course, she had her younger sisters. But sometimes when she was alone through the night she longed for something more. For someone to hold and cherish her. To show her what it was to experience pleasure.

Winding her arms around his neck, she flicked her tongue against his own as he'd done to her. Satisfaction filled her when he moaned in reply. She'd never been so bold before.

But when the distant tinkling of laughter reached her ears, reality returned in a blink. Wrenching herself away from him, Holly took several steps backward, her breathing coming in ragged breaths. Oh goodness, what had she been thinking. What had she been doing? She'd nearly been caught once tonight. She couldn't afford to be caught again.

Holly had always prided herself on her sensible nature and level-headedness. But kissing Michael and clinging to him like he was her life-line, was certainly not sensible and was definitely not level-headed. In fact, it was completely out of character. What was wrong with her?

He must think her an absolute wanton. It took her several moments to muster up the courage to glance up at him, only to find him staring at her like a hawk.

There was an intensity in his gaze that she found

compelling instead of fearful, and if not for the pulsing of the vein at his neck and his rapid breathing, Holly may have thought him entirely unaffected by their kiss.

A distinctly feminine part of her was glad the kiss had rattled him too, even if that was perhaps too strong a word for it as Michael certainly wasn't one to be rattled by anything, especially not by a kiss. He'd probably kissed hundreds of women before her. Though that was most likely exaggerating the number, or maybe not. The man looked like a darkly sinful Apollo, so much so that Holly doubted there would be many women who could resist his charms.

Herself now, unfortunately, included in that number.

Good gracious, she was already back to thinking of him as Michael, too. She must remember the proprieties, more so to keep a distance between them, than any true concern over such matters. For the last thing she intended to do was become enamored with a rake. That would be foolhardy and idiotic, not to mention she had far more important concerns to occupy her time with. Such as earning a living to support her sisters with, which certainly was not being accomplished by kissing the man in front of her.

Suddenly, she felt awkward and unsure. He undoubtedly didn't even realize that was her first proper kiss. Or perhaps he did and her ruse would be over?

"Come along then." Michael offered her his arm. "I shall escort you home."

"I do not need an escort." She ignored his hand and continued out the door and down the hallway toward the main ballroom. She was infinitely aware that Michael was following closely behind her, and though she did wish to return home, the last thing she wanted right then was to be trapped in the small confines of a carriage with him.

That would spell disaster, particularly after the kiss they'd just shared as Holly rather suspected that she'd throw herself at him and make a complete idiot of herself in the bargain. More so than she already had, which was completely unacceptable, especially from her. She stopped just shy of the main hallway and turned back to face him. "I thank you for the offer, though as you're aware now, I'm a widow and am perfectly capable of finding my own way home."

His eyes narrowed and his jaw clenched. "Widow or not, I intend to see you home safely."

"Surely you are not worried I shall be accosted on the way home?" she said, watching as a look almost akin to guilt flashed across his face. "Why do you suddenly look as guilty as sin? What on earth is going on, Michael?"

But in a blink the expression was gone, only to be replaced by a completely straight face. "Nothing is wrong. I promised your brother I'd look out for you, is all."

"Why *now*, are you suddenly trying to look out for me?"

"What do you mean by that?" he asked, confusion clouding his face.

"Edward has been dead for two years. Why the sudden interest in my welfare?"

It seemed as if he was about to say something, but then closed his mouth and cleared his throat. "I've only returned from the Crimea a few months ago and I admit that I purposefully stayed away as I didn't want my own reputation to damage yours."

"You don't seem to be overly worried about that now."

"You're a widow now." He cast her a veiled glance. "It doesn't matter if you are seen with me. And I suppose I also didn't worry overly before as I thought the dowry would be enough to ensure you married well. I never thought your husband would not request it."

Holly felt like laughing or perhaps crying. He had no idea

that it was the blasted dowry he'd bestowed on her and her sisters that had caused them to flee from their home in the first place. Well, one of the main reasons. But she'd never tell him that. Michael might be many things, and a rake was certainly one of them. Yet he'd never been a cruel or mean person and if he discovered that his gesture of *looking after* them had actually created the catalyst that they were still hiding from, he'd feel wretched. And Holly didn't want him to feel that way as it wasn't his fault that her uncle was a jackass.

"Michael, I have essentially been looking after my family since my mother died while giving birth to Daphne over seventeen years ago. And then when my father died do you think it was Edward that took care of everything? Of course not! He went off to the war and died in a stupid bar fight before he even got to fight on the front lines. Who do you think it was that looked after everyone then? Who still looks after everyone?"

Michael was silent for a good minute. "I didn't mean to imply that you couldn't take care of yourself." He dragged a hand through his thick mane of hair once again, in a gesture she was beginning to find annoyingly endearing. "You're one of the most competent women I've ever met."

Holly could feel a slight flush begin to creep across her cheeks. Michael had never complimented her over anything before, preferring to trade insults with her.

But then his next words ruined the warm fuzzy feeling she'd been experiencing.

"You're bloody bossy and stubborn to go with it, of course, but you're competent nonetheless."

"What exactly is your point then Michael? Apart from naming all of my faults."

He exhaled harshly. "You're a widow now Holly, that means you are fair game to a lot of men. I'm just trying to protect you from them because they'll try to take advantage of you. You can trust me on that."

"And what about from you, Michael?" She raised her chin slightly. "You were the one in there kissing me. Not any other men. How are you going to protect me from yourself?"

He shook his head and sighed. "Honestly? I don't know. The kiss was a mistake. I will protect you from other men, and from myself."

She'd never seen this side of Michael before. Gone was the confidence and arrogance that was usually clinging to him like a second skin. In their place, was a stark honesty in his expression that was compelling, even though a voice inside her head was warning her to run as far away from him as she could.

"Besides, you're obviously involved in something all the way up to your pretty little neck if what you were doing in Pembrook's study was any indication," Michael continued. "So clearly, you do need protecting."

"Not from you I don't." She knew with a deep certainty that this man would break her heart if she let him too close. "And you have no need to worry, I'm actually here with Lady Bosworth and her new husband. They will see me safely home. Look, there they are now." And thank goodness they were getting their cloaks which meant they would be leaving shortly, but oddly enough the Duke of Huntington and the Marquis of St. Giles were with them.

"It seems to be a night filled with rakes, does it not?" she mused aloud.

"What do you mean?" Michael asked, his eyes following to where she was now pointing. "Those damn bastards!"

Holly tilted her chin up to study the thunderous expression crossing his brow as he looked upon the small group in the distance. "I thought they were friends of yours?"

"They were until a moment ago," he announced, crossing

his arms over his chest, a mutinous expression on his altogether too handsome face.

Something was obviously going on, and Holly was immediately intrigued, despite her misgivings. "I shall have to have Lady Bosworth introduce me to them, then." Michael swore behind her as she strode over to her friends and the two libertines she'd never thought to meet in person. After all, in reality she was simply Miss Holly Jenkins, with no real wealth or family connections to warrant an introduction to two of London's most infamous and titled bachelors. Her sisters would relish hearing the details of such an occurrence. Well, at least, her youngest sister Daphne would. Violet might be a different story.

A short while later, after being introduced to the two men by an entirely reluctant Lady Bosworth, Holly found herself the center of not only Michael's attentions, albeit there was a fierce scowl creasing his brow, but also the Devil Duke and St. Giles were staring at her with unabashed interest in their eyes.

How very odd. Not that Holly was at all worried over the situation. Regardless of the men's disreputable reputations she couldn't imagine she was in any peril of being seduced by the two bounders. Although, the way St. Giles and the Devil Duke were looking at her did give her pause. Their expressions were seductively predatory. Though that was most likely how they normally appeared. She had to stifle her laughter at the thought.

A part of her was disappointed that Michael wasn't looking at her in the same manner as his friends, in fact, he wasn't looking at her at all now but instead glaring ferociously at his companions almost as if he were jealous, which was certainly not the case.

Bizarre behavior from him indeed. The whole evening had been odd, actually.

But before she could examine it any further, Lady Bosworth was complaining of a headache and her husband was whisking her and Holly toward the entrance hall and away from the three men before she could even gather her wits.

She glanced back over her shoulder to see all three men staring after her. But there was only one man's gaze that she was aware of... Michael's.

"How odd was that?" Lady Bosworth whispered beside her as her husband swept them down the entrance stairs to the landing.

"Indeed!" Lord Bosworth agreed. "I do hope they haven't set their sights on you Mrs. Carlton. Terribly bad for one's reputation, a lady having anything to do with those three."

"Oh, I don't know about that." Lady Bosworth grinned. "Three of the Ton's most eligible bachelors interested in our Holly. I could think of worse things. And she is a widow which does allow her a lovely sort of freedom to do what she wants as long as she's semi-discreet about it."

The glare Lord Bosworth shot his wife was enough to make both women laugh.

However, the idea that Holly could potentially look at taking a lover because everyone thought her to be a widow was entirely intriguing...

Yes. Even Holly had to admit that having the attention of three such handsome and notorious men was somewhat flattering. Even if it had been for only a few minutes. Because she was not foolish enough to think she would be on any of their minds even now. No, already they would be prowling through the ballroom looking for someone else to take their interest. The thought was particularly depressing, knowing Michael would be in that mix too.

It was for the best though. The night had already proven that he was a distraction she could ill afford. She'd been on a mission tonight and had failed to retrieve the letters. Without those letters her dear friend could be not only socially ruined but financially too! Holly had to redirect her attention back onto her objective. Not on Michael Drake, the Viscount of Blackthorn. Even if the man did make her weak at the knees. Blast him!

CHAPTER 4

"HOLLY?" her sister Violet's voice sang out. "Were you expecting a visitor?"

Holly glanced up from the papers on her writing desk, only to see her sister gazing down to the street below, her brown eyebrow arched in puzzlement.

"No. Why? It's not Clare is it?" She didn't think she could stand to see the look of disappointment on her friend's face when she told her she'd been unsuccessful in retrieving the letters. Though they still had a chance at finding them at Pembrook's country manor. *If* Holly could wangle an invitation to the hunting weekend he was about to host.

"Um… No, it's not Clare." There was some hesitation in her sister's voice, which was most unlike Violet.

"Well, who is it then?"

Her youngest sister Daphne stood from where she'd been sitting reading and wandered over to where Violet was peering down at the front entrance. "Oh, he's very handsome, whoever he is."

The mere mention of the word handsome made her heart start to race as an image of Michael came straight to the forefront of her mind. Pushing back from her chair, Holly strode over to her sisters and peered down to the street below. She nudged them aside, but by the time she got a glimpse of whoever they had been discussing he'd disappeared under the portico of the front entrance.

The door bell sounded, and Holly jumped.

Her sisters noted her reaction and stared at her with unbridled curiosity.

"What is going on, Holly?" Violet asked. "Who is the gentleman at the door?"

Holly straightened and shrugged, trying to at least appear nonchalant as much as one could when every part of one's body was on edge. After last night all she'd been able to think of was Michael. Even her dreams had been filled with the man. Which was terrible considering she knew that there was no future for her with him. He was heir to an earldom. And heirs to earldoms didn't marry Miss Anybody, particularly one pretending to be a widow. They married young ladies of consequence and rank. Even attempting to think of a future with him was a waste of time.

She'd daydreamed of such a thing with him when she was younger, but now that she was supporting not only herself but her sisters too, she couldn't afford to be distracted once again with foolish dreams that would never become a reality.

Not that she would ever consider marrying a rake. She wasn't silly enough to do something so idiotic. Especially not with someone like Michael. He was the sort of man one could all too easily give one's heart to, and then without meaning to he'd shatter it into pieces when his eyes wandered across to another woman, as rake's eyes were bound to do.

"Well whoever it is, he certainly has a fine pair of horses," Daphne remarked, the green eyes that the three of them shared shining in excitement. "And did you see his carriage? Why it looked like it had gold plating on it."

"Um...excuse me? Mrs. Carlton?" Their housekeeper, Mrs. O'Dowd spoke from the doorway. "Um...the um...the Duke of Huntington is here to call upon you."

Mrs. O'Dowd looked rattled, standing there wringing her hands in her skirts, a foreign expression of nervousness shining in her eyes.

"The Devil Duke is here? Calling on you, Holly?" Violet exclaimed, her mouth hanging agape for a moment. "Oh, my Lord, what happened last night? You only mentioned seeing Lord Blackthorn, not the Devil Duke, too."

"I met him briefly," Holly replied in a harsh whisper. "How was I to know he'd come calling?"

"Someone else is arriving too," Daphne's voice sang out from the window.

Violet rushed back to the window. "Good gracious, it's the Marquis of St. Giles." She swiveled back to Holly, her eyes narrowing. "Is he coming to call on you also? You need to start talking, sister!"

"Um, Mrs. Carlton?" Mrs. O'Dowd interrupted. "What about the duke? I can't really just leave a duke standing in the entrance hall, can I?"

Holly felt like she had to be dreaming. Nothing else made sense, even though she knew it was all too real to be a dream. But it did beg the question, what were two of London's most infamous lords doing visiting her? Her, a supposed widow, whom they'd only just met last night. It made no sense. "Send him in Mrs. O'Dowd. And the Marquis too, once he arrives. And then please bring us in some tea and cakes, I suppose. If that's what one even serves to men of their rank."

"They'll probably need brandy," Violet remarked. "I think we all will after today."

Holly for once, wholeheartedly agreed with her sister.

"You probably should send in Lord Blackthorn too," Daphne added, her voice filled with delight. "Considering he's just shown up too."

"Michael is here?" The latest news made her head start pounding. Three of the Ton's most notorious and eligible bachelors visiting her? Something was not right with the situation.

"*Michael?*" Violet's voice was completely unimpressed as she glanced over at Holly. "You haven't seen him in years, yet you're calling him by his first name? What really happened last night?"

She all but rounded on her sister. "Nothing happened! It's just, well, childhood habits can be hard to break. Now come on the both of you, sit before they get here."

Violet reluctantly took a seat on the chaise longue, while Daphne enthusiastically hurried across from the window and followed suit.

"Fancy having a duke, a marquis, *and* a viscount come to visit you, Holly," Daphne enthused, her blonde curls bobbing wildly in tune with her excited chatter. "How exciting! I simply cannot wait to tell my friends."

"Don't you dare! The gossip will already be fierce if others have seen them arriving here," Holly whispered. "And perhaps you shouldn't even be here, Daphne. You're having your coming out next year, and I have no intention of your reputation being tarnished even in the slightest."

"Sound advice," a deep voice echoed from the doorway.

Holly gulped, jumping up from her seat and turning toward the doorway. The Devil Duke was standing there, filling the entire doorway with his frame and wearing a wicked grin on his ridiculously handsome face, but thankfully he didn't look bothered by Holly's comment.

"I apologize, Your Grace," Holly rushed out. "I meant no insult."

The duke walked into the room over to Holly. He picked up her hand and slowly bent forward. "None taken, Mrs. Carlton," he replied, before placing a deft kiss on her knuckles.

Even Holly had to admit that the man's sensuality was potent, though it didn't affect her physically like Michael's touch had. He looked to be the same height as Michael, and like Michael had blue eyes but darker midnight black hair, and though both men were dashingly handsome, there were shadows within the duke's eyes that weren't in Michael's. Almost like a wall, protecting the duke from revealing anything truly about himself.

"You bastard," Michael's voice growled from behind.

Both Holly and the duke glanced up toward the doorway. Standing there, glaring at the Huntington with murder in his eyes was Michael, after having pushed St. Giles out of the way, with the man cursing loudly behind him.

Holly thought she might have laughed, if she hadn't been so confounded by their unexpected visit and odd behavior.

She could all but feel the energy crackling off Michael and for a minute she was worried he was actually going to start something with the duke, right here in her sitting room. What had gotten into him? He was acting stupidly possessive, and if it had anything to do with that promise he made her brother, she thought she might just scream. "Would one of you mind telling me what on earth is going on here?"

For safety sake, she took a step to stand in between the duke and Michael. She had a feeling that she might need to keep Michael from charging the man.

"I don't know about these two," St. Giles said as he stepped through the doorway past Michael. "But I've come to call upon you, Mrs. Carlton, and pay my unreserved respects."

"You have?" She could hear the disbelief in her own voice.

"We all have," Huntington agreed, seemingly unconcerned about Michael's upset. "Unfortunately, though it appears we all have terrible timing, bothering you three lovely ladies all at once." He smiled at her two sisters and Holly could not resist rolling her eyes when both Violet and Daphne sighed in unison.

Really, she thought she'd taught them better than to be taken in by a scoundrel and his smile. Though he wasn't just any scoundrel, and it wasn't just any smile. He was the Devil Duke and women fell at his feet all the time, and with that devastating smile of his, she could somewhat understand why. But if he thought to use his charms on her or her sisters, he was sorely mistaken.

Even now, she could feel the fierce need to protect them from him start to rise within her.

"Perhaps it would be best if we call on you another day," the duke continued, his eyes flicking past her to Michael, who hadn't said anything further. "Individually though."

Holly's gaze darted between all three men. "Yes, perhaps that would be best." She got the feeling that the sooner she could get them all out of her house, the better. Then, she could make some enquiries and find out what was really going on with the three of them.

She was slightly astounded when the duke picked up her hand and kissed it again, almost as if he were baiting Michael, who bristled behind her like a great hulking bear, while St. Giles tried to stifle a chuckle. Holly felt like she was in some sort of theater production but had lost her script; not quite knowing what was going on but knowing that something definitely was. Something involving her.

"Until next time, Mrs. Carlton." The duke winked at her, before bowing toward her sisters. "Ladies." Then, without a backward glance, he strode past her and Michael out the doorway, his boots clipping on the parquet flooring, fading gradually as he walked down the hallway to the entrance.

"Mrs. Carlton." St. Giles bowed toward her, though seemed to think better of kissing her hand, before he too turned and strode out the door.

Michael began to bow but Holly snaked out her hand and grabbed his arm. "Oh no you do not! Don't you dare think you are leaving until you tell me what is going on!"

Her sisters gasped, while Michael simply stared at her, his eyes giving nothing away. "It is as the duke explained."

Holly narrowed her eyes on him and began to tap her foot. She had to do something to redirect her frustration. "What an amazing coincidence that you all just happened to call upon me today."

"Yes. Amazing." Michael nodded, the aggressiveness that had been radiating from him a moment ago while the other two men had been present, dissipating like it had never been.

Oh, the man frustrated her to no end! "Violet. Daphne. Please leave us, now."

Violet gasped. "We can't do that! You can't be left alone with someone of his reputation." She looked somewhat sheepishly toward Michael, but crossed her hands over her chest in defiance. "Apologies, Lord Blackthorn, but it's the truth," she directed toward him.

Briefly Holly smiled. It was nice to know her sister was being protective. "I shall be fine, Violet. I am a *widow*, after all. My reputation shall not be tarnished from a few moments alone with Lord Blackthorn."

"But—"

"No buts, Violet," Holly quickly interrupted her. She didn't think Violet would purposefully reveal the truth, but her sister sometimes got rather passionate about things. "Please, Violet. I need to speak with him alone, just for a moment."

"Yes, come along, sister." Daphne walked over to Violet and took her hand, forever the peacemaker between her two older sisters. "Holly shall be fine for we shall be waiting right outside in the corridor." Her eyes narrowed upon Michael, in what Holly guessed was a warning for him to behave.

She did love her sisters, even if they exasperated her sometimes.

Reluctantly, Violet nodded and followed Daphne to the door. "A moment only."

They both stepped out into the hallway, shutting the door closed behind them, and leaving Holly alone in the room with Michael.

For a minute, they simply stood there staring at each other.

"Daphne has grown since I last saw her, though Violet is still as ferocious as usual," Michael said, breaking the silence.

"Yes, I suppose so." The last time Michael had seen Daphne, she had been fifteen and she had shot up in height and lost the trappings of youth in the two years since. "What are you really doing here, Michael?" she asked. "Because I truly doubt it's to actually pay me a call."

He looked flustered for a second, but only for a second before a mask of implacability settled over his face again. "I told you. I intend to ensure you are looked after. I prom—"

"Yes, yes. The promise you made to my brother. I know!" Frustration welled inside her. "You have no idea of how that damn promise of yours has impacted us over the years. None at all."

"What do you mean by that?" His eyes narrowed down upon her and she could see his mind replaying her words.

But she couldn't explain anything to him. If she did he would know the truth, and that could potentially jeopardize her sisters' reputations, which she would never do. Besides, knowing Michael he would probably feel guilty if he knew

Holly had been forced to flee with her sisters from their childhood home after Edward's death. Forced to pretend she was a widow so her uncle couldn't find her, or at least if he did, would have no power to compel her to marry his son. "It doesn't matter." She swept her arms around the room before stepping to stand directly in front of him. "As you can see, I am fine. Perfectly fine."

"Yes," he agreed. "Your husband obviously provided well for you in his will."

Holly felt like laughing. He had no idea of what it had been like in the first year after her father's death. "Yes, Harold was good to me. His estate still provides me an income which I make good use of." It wasn't too much of a lie, considering she earned her own income.

But his eagle-eyed stare resting on her own, was getting uncomfortable. Holly was certain if he stared at her longer he'd see the lie in her story. She needed to get him out of there. "If you don't intend on telling me the truth of your visit today, then perhaps you should leave."

"Actually, there was another reason for my visit."

"Yes?" she prompted.

"I want you to tell me why you were breaking into Lord Pembrook's safe last night?" he replied.

"So that's why you're here!" It made sense. Though the other men visiting still didn't.

"Are you in trouble?" Michael all but demanded.

"I most certainly am not." Trust a man to jump to such a conclusion.

"Then tell me what you were doing picking his safe," Michael said. "Because your hobby has turned damned dangerous."

Holly felt like shaking the man. "I cannot tell you."

"Do you not trust me?"

"It's not about trust," she replied. "I simply cannot tell you." It was not her secret to share.

"Then you do not trust me," he replied gruffly, before turning toward the door. "I shall leave then."

She didn't know what came over her, but she reached out and grabbed his arm. "Wait. It's not that! I would be breaking someone's confidence if I said anything."

Michael swiveled around to face her and their eyes locked. And suddenly everything melted away but him and the stormy blue of his gaze as a searing heat flew between them, burning in its intensity.

She didn't know who started it, and she suspected it may well have been her, but suddenly they were kissing in a frenzy, their bodies pressed against each other, their tongues and lips dancing in a rhythm of unrestrained passion.

She tasted like peaches and cream, and Michael couldn't get enough of her. He deepened his kiss, flicking his tongue against her own, thrilling as her heartbeat leaped wildly against his chest in response.

There was no coquettish teasing or falseness from Holly. She was opening herself fully to his kiss and Michael adored it. He could only imagine what it would be like to pleasure her. To hear her breathless gasps as she orgasmed around his shaft, while he pumped himself inside her until they climaxed together.

He knew it would be an experience unlike any he'd had before, which was saying something. But there was a quality about Holly that had always been compelling, as much as he'd fought against the feeling for years. Learning she was a widow however, had been like unlocking a tantalizing gate that had always been forever out of reach.

But she wasn't out of reach now. Where once she'd been completely off limits, now she was available. Like some sort of forbidden fruit he'd been wanting to taste for years but hadn't dared. A fruit he was desperately craving.

But damn it! He'd promised Edward he'd look out for her. How could he in good conscience do so, while seducing her? He truly was a bastard sometimes to even think of doing such a thing.

Especially when he was responsible for her brother's death. She'd never forgive him if she ever found out. The look of hatred that would replace the passionate haze in her emerald eyes was enough to send a cold shard of dread through him.

Holly Jenkins—or Carlton as she was now—was off limits, even if she was a widow. Hell, she'd always been off limits. She'd been his best-friends younger sister, and one didn't dally with one's friend's sister. He might be a cad in some respects but not with that. Part of the reason he'd stayed away from her. He'd always been aware of her but knew nothing would come of it.

Reluctantly, he broke his lips away from hers, every inch of his body rebelling with the action.

"I'm sorry." His gruff voice broke the silence. "I shouldn't have done that." He had to get this unaccountable lust firmly under control before there was no going back.

Holly appeared adorably befuddled as she blinked and licked her full lips. Lips that had been ravished and were begging for more.

Michael nearly groaned aloud, battling to restrain his hands from literally reaching out and pulling her against him again. He took a step away from her and strode over to the window.

Space. He needed to put some space between them before he lost all measure of his self-control.

He'd always prided himself on his restraint, but with Holly it had completely deserted him. Instead of the notorious rake he was known to be, he was acting like some silly, infatuated schoolboy who couldn't keep his hands to himself. A situation that was entirely unacceptable. He had to leave now before his reticence crumbled.

"Yes, I, um...well I'm sorry too," Holly stammered, her eyes darting everywhere but at him.

A dusky rose flush spread over her cheeks and Michael found himself enchanted, wondering if she was blushing anywhere else?

He shook his head in disgust. What was wrong with him? He was acting a fool. "I'll see myself out," he managed to mumble as he stalked past her heading directly for the door. He wrenched it open and both Violet and Daphne stumbled forward into him, screeching in surprise. Balancing them back on their feet, he saw that blushing was clearly a trait amongst the Jenkins' ladies, as the girls' faces were flaming at being discovered eavesdropping.

And for some reason the situation amused him and he laughed aloud, which was something he hadn't done in a very long time. "Ladies," he said, bowing to them both briefly before heading down the hallway.

"Don't think this is the end of you telling me what is really going on Michael Drake!" Holly's voice yelled down the passage. "For I fully intend to get the truth out of you!"

Michael paused and looked back over his shoulder. She was standing in the doorway, her eyes lit with determination as she glared down the hallway at him. She looked bloody gorgeous, but rather than fear at the possibility of seeing her again, he felt anticipation. "Perhaps when you tell me your secret, I shall tell you mine." He winked at her, before turning around and walking to the entrance hall.

He took his hat from the housekeeper and couldn't help

but grin when the words, 'Oh, that damn man! He frustrates me to no end!' floated down the passage.

The housekeeper cringed. "I'm sorry, my lord. Miss Holly gets rather passionate at times."

Michael shrugged and smiled at the woman while donning his hat. The woman had no idea. "It's fine, I've experienced her ire many times over the years and I imagine it won't lessen in the future."

"Oh, you have?" She looked confused but smiled nonetheless. "Well, have a good day then."

"I intend to," he replied. The first thing he was going to do was make some enquiries as to what Holly had been up to snooping in Pembrook's safe. Because knowing Holly, she would keep looking for whatever it was she hadn't found and was bound to get into trouble in the process. When did she not? And if she thought he would leave her to do so, she was sorely mistaken, the stubborn chit.

As he strode down the footpath toward his carriage, suddenly Michael felt lighter and filled with purpose. He hadn't felt that way since after Edward died, not even during the war. Perhaps finally things weren't going to be so bad after all.

CHAPTER 5

"It is just as I suspected!" Holly cried, as she read the note once again. After the chaos earlier that morning she'd immediately sent out some letters seeking information.

"What are you referring to?" Violet asked, peering up from the pages of her book.

Holly glanced around the library, making sure that Daphne wasn't anywhere in the vicinity. Though she didn't like to keep things from her youngest sister, she was still just a girl, and somethings were better off being kept secret from her, as Daphne did tend to blurt out information, before thinking better of it.

Thankfully Violet was much more like Holly and could be relied upon to keep a secret. "I knew that those bounders were up to something!" Holly folded up the paper, before stuffing it into her skirt pocket and marching over to the hat stand. She plucked her teal bonnet from off the hook.

"Your callers from this morning?" Violet guessed. Her sister was always very quick to catch on about things.

"Yes," she replied, slamming the hat on her head and tying

up the strings. "I sent a letter to Lady Winthrup asking her if she'd heard anything relating to the three men."

"Well, Mabel Winthrup is the biggest gossip in London, if anyone would know anything it's bound to be her," Violet surmised. "And by your response I'm guessing she knows what the men are up to."

"Indeed, she does." One could always rely on Mabel to know the latest on dit, the woman was a veritable fount of information. "Apparently, the men have a wager going between the three of them, worth three thousand pounds as to who can seduce me first!"

"What?" Violet's book fell forgotten in her lap. "You cannot be serious!"

"Oh, I am," she said, pulling out the note from Lady Winthrup and walking it over to Violet. She pushed it into her sister's somewhat stunned hand, before returning to the stand and retrieving her cloak from it.

Violet read the short missive quickly. "How dare they do such a thing!"

"Actually, I'm rather glad of it. It's very fortuitous timing." Holly swung the cloak over her shoulders.

"Fortuitous timing?" Violet sounded outraged. "Are you serious, Holly? Are you not furious that they've only been paying you attention because of a bet?"

"Not in the slightest," Holly replied. And it was true, well except for Michael's role in it. She could care less about the Devil Duke or St. Giles chasing after her because of a bet, in fact she was somewhat flattered by their attention, especially as she knew she'd never succumb to their charms. What did hurt though, was that Michael had only been seeking her out because of it. After their past together she'd expected a bit more from him.

She never should have let him kiss her. She knew what he was like, though a part of her had thought perhaps she meant something more to him than all of the other ladies he'd kissed. More the fool she. Though it had awakened in her a hunger and curiosity to know what it was like to experience passion.

For so long, she'd placed the needs and wants of everyone else above her own. It was time to place her own needs first for a change.

Not that she was about to confess any of that to her sister, although she suspected Violet had already guessed or at least imagined what had been going on in the sitting room that morning between Holly and Michael, her sister was after all three-and-twenty and rather clever too.

"Well I would be furious!" Violet declared, standing and striding over to Holly while waving the note around like a flag. "And I'd be surprised if deep down you weren't either."

"What I am, is excited." Holly plucked the note out of her sister's hand and returned it to her pocket.

"Excited?" There was disbelief in Violet's voice. "You're excited that you're essentially a piece of meat in a wager between three scoundrels? Have you gone mad, sister?"

Holly briefly considered the question. Perhaps she had, though she was always one to believe the glass was half full. "I'm going to use the bet for my own purposes."

"What do you mean?" Violet's eyes narrowed. "You don't actually intend to be seduced by Blackthorn, do you?"

She could already feel the blush staining her cheeks at the suggestion. "Why would you immediately say him? The other two are nearly as handsome." Hopefully her sister wouldn't realize Holly hadn't answered the question, because after a great deal of reflection, Holly had decided that she did want to be seduced by him. She was wasn't getting any younger, and it was highly unlikely that she'd ever have a chance to have an illicit affair again.

And if she was going to have an intimate liaison with

anyone, Michael would be the one to do so with, as not only was she greatly attracted to him, but he would be well versed in how to pleasure her. The very thought sent a decidedly wicked thrill all the way down to her toes.

It was time to think of her own needs. She deserved to at least have some memories of excitement and satisfaction to hold on to.

"Please," Violet scoffed, placing her hands on the cream-colored gown covering her hips. "St. Giles is by far the handsomest of the lot. But why Blackthorn, you ask?" A smug little grin crossed her rosy lips. "Anyone only had to look at you both to see the attraction literally simmering between the two of you."

"You exaggerate the situation, Violet." Holly buttoned up the cloak, refusing to be goaded by her sister.

"No. I don't," Violet replied. "I feel it prudent to remind you, Holly, that you're not actually a widow, which clearly these men don't know or they'd be avoiding you like the plague."

"I'm well aware of that fact, Violet." A sister could be a right royal pain sometimes. "You can rest assured, I have no intention of allowing anyone to take liberties with me against my will. Most especially not Blackthorn." Violet didn't need to know that Holly fully intended to give Michael permission to seduce her.

Though she did feel a bit guilty about possibly misleading her sister. But there were some things that simply couldn't be shared.

"Then where are you going at this hour? It's nearly midnight, Holly."

"I'll explain it to you when I get back, I promise." She squeezed her sister's hands before striding over to the door. "I should be back before the morning, but just in case I'm not, do make sure Daphne gets to her lessons."

"They're dangerous men, Holly," Violet warned. "Most especially, Blackthorn."

"He would never hurt me, sister."

"Not physically," Violet agreed. "It's more your heart I'm worried for."

Holly took a deep breath and paused with her hand on the door knob. That was her fear too, though she'd nearly convinced herself it would be fine. "My heart is quite safe, trust me." She could see the concern in her sister's eyes and for once was touched rather than vexed. "You know I need to help Lady Clare retrieve those letters. Not only do we need the funds her commission will pay, but she's too kind and decent to let a scoundrel ruin her."

Violet sighed. "So, whatever you're up to has something to do with that?"

She nodded. "I need to get to Pembrook's country manor and all three of those dolts have invitations to his hunting party this coming weekend."

Violet's eyes widened in understanding. "Oh, you are fiendishly clever, Holly."

"Time to make their bet work in my favor, I think. Don't you?" In more ways than one.

The two women grinned at each other, before Violet raced up and gave her a quick hug. "Just guard your heart, sister. I fear Lord Blackthorn would unintentionally tear it to shreds if you let him."

Holly nodded, before turning around and hurrying down the hallway to the front door. Violet's worries were unfounded as Holly had no intention of giving him her heart. Her body perhaps, but never her heart. She'd already lost her father and brother. The two most important men in her life. Her heart couldn't withstand falling hard for a man and then losing him too as of course was bound to happen if she gave her heart to Michael.

No. She wouldn't permit that. But that didn't mean she couldn't allow herself to experience the decadence of his touch.

After all, she was six and twenty and well and truly on the shelf. This could be the last time she had an opportunity to know what all the fuss of a man bedding a woman was about. And if it was as pleasurable as his kisses, well then, she was open to giving it a try. Though she would never be stupid enough to entrust her heart with a rake, something Michael was, and would always be. Leopards never changed their spots in the end.

CHAPTER 6

THE FOG outside the window slowly crept up the buildings, cloaking everything in a white haze until it all seemed to be fading away into nothingness, and for some reason Michael felt he was getting a glimpse of his own future.

He sighed and sunk back further into his leather chair, staring at the roaring flames of the hearth. Perhaps the fire would dispel the odd mood he'd been in for most of the day. But it was no use. A sense of inevitability clung to him, heavily. Which try as he might, he couldn't shake.

After leaving Holly's house in the morning, following that farce of a visit with those buffoons he called friends, his spirits had been high. Probably the highest they'd been in years, but then reality had hit him like a brick when he'd been summoned to his father's townhouse shortly after. The visit reminding him amply, of how ludicrous it was to think he could be happy. That he could possibly lead a normal life.

What a fool he was.

And now here he was in his study, trying to drown his sorrows with whiskey and he couldn't even do that. He was not only a fool but an incompetent one, to boot.

A prickle of awareness crept up his neck and instantly Michael knew he wasn't alone.

"You're not going to try to rob *my* safe now, are you?" He said aloud to his previously empty study. Though he couldn't see her, he could sense her.

The feminine huff of annoyance echoed loudly through the room, originating from behind him toward the doors to the patio. "How did you know I was here? Let alone that it was me?"

He smiled, in spite of his glumness. Seemed like Holly could always lift his mood. "Fresh linen and rosewater."

From the corner of his eye she moved into view, wearing a tailored black cloak over an emerald green dress, with a matching green bonnet sporting some leaves throughout the lace netting of it.

"What do you mean linen and rosewater?" she asked.

"*Fresh* linen, actually," he replied, stretching his legs out in front of him. "You smell of fresh linen and rosewater. A combination I've recently grown rather fond of. That's how I knew you were here."

She pursed her lips as her gaze went from him to the bottle of whiskey and the glass sitting on the table to his right. "How many of those have you had?"

"Not enough." He reached forward and picked up his glass, before taking a healthy swallow. "That's for certain."

Wandering over to the seat across from him Holly sat down, the hoop of her skirt compressing in the small confines of the space.

"Some of the garden appears to have gotten into your millinery," he pointed out.

A mutinous expression crossed that beautiful face of hers, but her hands quickly reached up and swatted some of the greenery from her hat. Oh yes, she was definitely miffed and he only wanted her all the more.

He was going insane.

"You could have used the front door," he decided to mention. "Probably easier than traipsing through the back-garden and picking the balcony lock, I dare say."

"And be seen entering your residence alone and at this hour?" She scoffed. "I'm not an idiot."

"Oh, I don't know about that. Traipsing about London on your own at this hour seems fairly idiotic to me." He held up his glass to her. "But where are my manners? Would you like a drink?"

"Yes, actually I would," she replied, rendering him momentarily speechless.

Reaching over, she plucked the glass from his hands and took a healthy swallow before handing it back to him.

A moment later she started coughing.

"Good gracious, what is that stuff?" she choked out. "It burns."

Michael grinned. "Bloody good, isn't it? But I doubt you've come to talk to me about Scotch whiskey. Want to tell me why you're visiting me in the dead of night, and how for that matter, did you know I'd be home?" He'd usually be at his club at this time of the night, but after his encounter with his father all he'd felt like doing was being alone.

"Lucky, I suppose." She shrugged. "I thought I'd try here first and then if I had no luck, I was going to try your club next, and then if you weren't there I was going to find your friends and see if they knew where you were."

"My friends?" He could literally start to feel his blood heating.

"Yes," she concurred. "I thought surely the Devil Duke or St. Giles would know your whereabouts or could at least point me in the right direction."

"And tell me this," he'd dropped his voice to nearly a whisper. "How were you getting around to all of these places at this hour of the evening, or rather morning? And visiting notorious bachelors' residences into the bargain!"

"By hackney, my lord. How else? I don't own a carriage, like some."

There was a definite edge of sarcasm in her tone. "Did you not for one moment consider that the streets of London are dangerous? Especially for a woman as attractive as yourself, at this time of the morning!" He wasn't whispering anymore. In fact, his servants were probably wide awake with his yelling by now.

But Holly wasn't fussed as she continued to calmly sit there, plucking greenery and twigs from her cloak. "'Tis lucky I found you here then, isn't it, and as you can see I'm safe and sound."

"Not for much bloody longer," Michael growled.

She merely raised an eyebrow at him, much like one of his old governesses used to do in silent chastisement. "I know about the wager."

Her words stopped him cold. "The wager?"

"Yes, the wager." She smiled calmly at him. Too calmly, for someone who'd only just found out about such a thing. "The one where whoever is the first to seduce me wins the three-thousand-pounds. *That* wager."

Damn it. She did know. "I can explain."

"There's no need to."

Michael narrowed his eyes upon her. There was a calmness and composure to her that he certainly would not have expected her to possess upon discovering the wager. "Are you *not* upset?" He braced himself for an outburst of the anger that was sure to come, but all she did was shrug.

"It's actually quite handy."

"Handy?" He wondered if his voice sounded as perplexed as he felt. Perhaps Holly was furious, more furious than he thought possible. Although she didn't seem at all furious. Not in the slightest. Her lack of anger was rather disturbing.

"Yes. You see, I've come to offer you a proposition. One that I think will meet both of our needs."

"A proposition?" He nearly stammered over the words. "God help me."

"Yes, a proposition. Now, are you certain you haven't drunk too much?" She looked suspiciously down at the whiskey bottle, then back up to him. "I do want you to be sober enough to remember what you're agreeing to."

"Damn it, I'm sober. Ridiculously sober at the moment, unfortunately!" he exclaimed. Staying here, alone, with her in arm's reach and talking about a proposition was a very bad idea. A very bad idea, indeed.

She tilted her chin to the side, looking entirely unimpressed. "There's no need to bite my head off. I'm simply making certain."

"Holly, will you please get to the damn point." He ran a hand through his hair and had to make an effort to calm down. Jumping to his feet, he began pacing across the room. Anything to try to alleviate the sudden restlessness he was feeling.

"You know," she pointed out. "I should be the one vexed over the wager, not you."

"Holly…" he growled, pausing for a heartbeat before continuing to pace up and back. "Please just get to the point."

"Well, you obviously wish to win your bet, considering your behavior toward me in the last two days. And I…. I need an invitation to Lord Pembrook's hunting party this weekend at his country estate."

"And?" Michael prompted, feeling somewhat confused.

"Isn't it obvious?" she enthused. "I shall agree to be your, what was it called in your wager? Your mistletoe mistress I believe? Well, I shall agree to that, and then you can take me to Pembrook's this weekend."

"Let me guess." Michael stopped pacing and turned to face her. "So you can search his safe?"

Holly grinned at him. "Exactly. You can win your wager and I will have a legitimate excuse for being there. Pembrook won't be at all suspicious if he thinks you and I are having a discreet liaison. Then while all you men are off hunting, and the ladies are busy doing whatever it is they do at a hunting party, I shall have ample time to search Pembrook's safe."

Michael took in a deep lungful of air, praying for patience right at that instant. "You have it all figured out, don't you?"

"I do." There was a definite sparkle of smugness in her gaze. "As I said, as long as we're circumspect, it's more than acceptable for a widow to be having a liaison with a lord. Happens all the time in society and shall work out quite well for us, don't you think?"

"All except the part about being my mistletoe mistress." With very deliberate steps, he walked over to where she sat and braced both of his hands on either side of her chair. Slowly, he lowered his head until it was but an inch from her own.

Holly gulped, a look of nervous anticipation replacing her confidence from a moment ago. "You didn't like that part?" she whispered.

"I don't cheat to win a wager."

"Who said anything about cheating?" There was a breathlessness to her words that enticed him. "I'm more than happy to fulfill my end of the bargain."

"Excuse me?" Michael was at a sudden loss for words. Was she actually suggesting what he thought she was? "You actually intend to have a liaison with me?"

"Yes, I do." She brought a hand up to his face and gently

stroked her fingers down his cheek. "I quite like the idea of being *your mistletoe* mistress."

"My mistletoe mistress?" Michael had to really listen to her words rather than think about her touch, which was sending thrills of delight through him.

"Yes. I think the arrangement will be quite suitable for both of us." There was a gleam of excitement in her gaze as she patted his cheek and then dropped her hand. "In fact, the possibilities of such a partnership are rather thrilling."

"They are?" Michael had to get his befuddled thoughts under control. He was losing control of the situation, and quickly. He sat back on the other chair facing her but putting some much-needed distance between him and her alluring scent.

"Indeed. You have access to many events that I do not, but as your special friend I shall be able to accompany you to them, which will make my work a great deal easier."

His head was definitely now pounding. "Your work, picking safes?"

Her brows drew together. "It's a little bit more than that. I'm stopping blackmailers and helping women to feel safe."

"Let me see if I understand you correctly." He paused and rubbed his temples, trying to get his thoughts in order. A darned hard thing to do in Holly's presence. "You wish to be my mistress, my actual mistress, mind you, so that you can gain access to balls to further your *work*? Do I have that quite correct?"

She smiled tremendously up at him. "You do. It is a satisfactory solution for both of us."

Michael rather doubted that, already imagining the inevitable trouble she would be certain to get herself caught up in, which he would invariably have to rescue her from. "Are you insane, woman?"

A scowl replaced the smile from a moment ago. "Actually, I think it's one of my more brilliant ideas."

"Only you would."

Holly stood and placed her hands on her hips, fire shining in her eyes. "Well, if you think it's so stupid then perhaps I should go and see if either the Devil Duke or St. Giles is more amenable to my proposal!"

His lips drew back in a snarl and he unfurled his frame to stand in front of her. "The hell you will!"

"Watch me, Michael Drake." Heat stained her cheeks as she poked him in the chest. "Just watch me!"

"The devil I will." He could literally feel a vein popping out in his neck. The woman was going to drive him insane. Absolutely insane. But as he stared down at her, both of them breathing heavily, suddenly his ire left him, swiftly replaced by a burning desire coursing through his blood. He wanted this woman, badly, and though he'd done all he could to resist her, his defenses were crumbling. "If you're so bloody determined to be someone's mistress, then you'll be mine. End of story." He desperately hoped Edward would forgive him, but what choice did he have when she was talking of being either Huntington's or St. Giles' mistress?

Holly crossed her arms over chest, a mutinous expression on her face. "Perhaps, I've now changed my mind!"

She looked so adorable standing there with her chin raised that all he wanted to do was sweep her into his arms and carry her up to his bed. And if she was set on this course of action, then the only way to fulfill his promise to her brother to protect her, was to agree to this damn proposal of hers. Even if guilt over Edward's death and keeping the truth from Holly, would eat him up inside. The woman was stubborn enough to do as she threatened. Really, the only way to protect her was to agree to this mad proposal of hers. There was no other way.

Now that his mind was made up, a sense of heady anticipation filled him. Holly was no longer a virgin that he had to protect from himself. She was a widow who had approached him. They could enjoy each other without limitations and as she said, provided they were indeed discreet, society wouldn't bat an eyelid.

And of course, when they decided to go their separate ways, he would ensure she was well taken care of for the rest of her life. She would never again want for anything. The promise he made to Edward would be amply fulfilled.

He pushed aside the niggle of guilt that whispered along the forefront of his mind.

If it wasn't himself having an affair with her, it would be the Devil Duke, and surely Edward would prefer Michael over Huntington, who went through women like wine. Holly deserved better than that.

The very idea was enough to firm his resolve.

"You haven't changed your mind though, have you?" he whispered, lowering his head down to her right ear. "Your body is all but begging me to touch you. To caress you. To seduce you. But I won't, not unless you tell me to."

"You won't?" She gulped, her eyes clouding over with passion.

"Most definitely not." He slowly started trailing kisses along the nape of her neck, down to her collarbone. She was so soft and smelt sweetly intoxicating. He breathed her scent in deeply, before he raised his head and stared straight into her eyes. "Are you going to be my mistletoe mistress, Holly?" God help them both.

CHAPTER 7

MICHAEL WAS RIGHT. Holly did want to be seduced by him.

Ever since he'd kissed her in Lord Pembrook's study the idea had been mulling about in her head, gathering momentum like a locomotive. And she'd been unable to shake the idea, or the sensation of his lips upon hers. The man certainly knew how to kiss. And now he was most likely going to be kissing her, a lot, and in many other places aside from her lips. The thought made her blush.

She probably was slightly insane for wanting to be his mistletoe mistress, but for her entire life she'd nearly always lived by the rules and comfortably within her limits.

Though the past two years had pushed those boundaries to their edges, she'd never placed herself in a situation she couldn't handle. And for once she wanted to take a risk. She wanted to know what it was like to fully experience being a woman, which as Michael's mistletoe mistress she would.

The very idea was both thrilling and daunting. Especially as he was under the impression she was an experienced widow. Perhaps she should tell him the truth? But if she did, he'd run a mile, which was the last thing she wanted. She needed him to get her into Pembrook's country estate, and besides, she was very firmly on the shelf so there was no harm in her discovering what it was to feel passion for once. After all, what did it matter that she was a virgin? It was her body and her choice. And society believed her to be a widow, so there would be nothing untoward about her carrying on a dalliance with Michael, provided they were discreet.

Certainly, he would be annoyed when he found out the truth. She knew that without a doubt. But, by then it would be too late and the deed would be done. For a moment guilt assailed her. Her inner voice was urging her to tell him, but she wasn't going to. She couldn't. Selfishly perhaps, she didn't want to risk him sending her away.

For so long Holly had always looked after everyone else, that it was time now for her to consider her own wants and needs. Time to be seduced by a man she was ridiculously attracted to.

"You will fulfill your end of the bargain?" she asked him, trying to not be distracted as his lips began to feather kisses down the nape of her neck.

His mouth paused against the beating pulse at her throat. "Yes, I will take you to Lord Pembrook's hunting party and to the other balls you need to go to," his voice was a rough whisper against her skin, sending a searing white heat down to her toes.

"Then I shall be your mistletoe mistress."

Before she could even gather her wits, he scooped her up into his arms and stalked from the room with her cradled against him.

Oh, good gracious, this was really going to happen. Holly could literally feel her heart pounding against her chest, but she wasn't at all scared. It was as if, for the first time, a deep sense of knowing filled her, nestled as she was in his arms.

Being with him felt so right that no matter what happened after, it was almost like it was destined.

A few moments later, after Michael had carried her up the silent staircase, he nudged open the door to what had to be his bedroom. There was a gigantic four-poster bed standing in the middle of the room, rather imposing with its thick sapphire colored, silk curtains tied back on each wooden post of the bed and a matching quilt lying on the mattress.

The thought of how many women he'd brought here into this very room flitted across her mind; but she firmly pushed it to the side. She was not going to let her fear of what was about to happen plant any seeds of doubt in her head. By goodness, she was going to enjoy this night with Michael.

He carried her across to the middle of the room and carefully deposited her on her feet. "Are you certain about this, Holly?" Michael asked, his fingers gently tilting up her chin until she was facing him. "I don't want you to have any regrets."

There was such concern and honesty in his features, that instantly Holly felt at ease. This was Michael. Deep down she knew, had always known, that she was safe with him. If she was going to lose her virginity to anyone, it might as well be to a man well versed in the art of lovemaking as he was. "I'm absolutely certain."

And to show him how certain she was, she reached up on tiptoes and wound her arms around his neck. Then, before she could think better of it, she pressed her lips against his.

There was a sizzle of energy between them.

Michael groaned and reached his hands around to cup her buttocks, pulling her in tightly against him as his mouth devoured hers. She could still taste the whiskey on his lips, but she could also taste him and had never wanted to feast on anything more.

Her gasp was smothered in his mouth, when she felt the length of him pressing against her belly. She'd never felt such a thing before. A sensation of wicked wantonness filled her as she reached her hand down and stroked him through the material of his trousers.

He was as hard as marble and suddenly she wanted nothing more than to get rid of the material between her hand and his manhood. She wanted to feel him against her.

With a boldness she hadn't known she possessed, her fingers reached into the waistband of his pants.

"Oh God, you're driving me insane woman, do you know that?" Michael all but moaned as her fingertips pushed under the material and danced along the edge of his shaft.

"I hope that's a good thing, in this context?" Holly grew even more daring as his breathing began to quicken the more she stroked the length of him.

"It is," he said with a half groan, half laugh. "But where are my manners? It would be ungentlemanly for me to have you doing all of the work."

"It would?"

"It certainly would." He winked at her and gently grabbed her hand, removing it from his pants.

"Oh." She pouted.

He chuckled and before she knew what he was about, his hands were expertly undoing the buttons of her cloak, before they moved onto the row of buttons along the back of her dress. Time felt frozen as he flicked each and every button open, slowly, one after another, parting her dress inch by agonizing inch.

Her whole body felt like it was on fire. She wanted him to tear away the clothing covering her flesh from his touch. Almost as if reading her mind, he began to slide her gown down over her body. She went to assist, but he stilled her hands.

"No need to rush," he teased. "We have all night and I intend to make use of every single minute. To pleasure you over and over again."

She was rather distracted by the feel of his hands plastered over her chemise as he slowly inched the dress down over her crinoline. "You do?"

"Oh, I certainly do," he said, and there was such a wicked promise in his words that Holly felt a thrill all over. He pulled lose the strings of her crinoline and it joined her dress on the floor. Then he began to unlace the stays at the front of her corset.

A grin flitted across her mouth. "Well please, do not let me stop you."

His smile joined her own as he flung the corset aside and scooped her up, before carrying her over to the bed. Deftly, he placed her onto the middle of it and quickly discarded his shirt, before laying down by her side.

Holly was certain she'd never seen a finer specimen of a man, than Michael. Not that she'd ever seen another man without his shirt on, but Michael was all smooth planes of muscle and hardness. She wanted to do nothing more, right at that moment, than to run her hands through the dark hairs covering his chest and follow the small trail all the way down to the waist band of his trousers.

"Goodness you're beautiful," she exclaimed.

Michael laughed. "Aren't I the one meant to be saying that to you?"

"By all means, feel free to," she responded. "But it's true. You're so deliciously masculine. All I want to do is touch you."

"Well, by all means…" He winked, using her own words back at her.

Holly shrugged. Why not? She wanted to know what it felt like to be with him, so she might as well experience as much as she could. With eagerness, she reached her hands up and glided them across his broad chest. His skin was so smooth but there was such strength underneath that sent a deep throb of desire through her.

He moaned as her hands started to go lower down his chest and brushed across his stomach. The sound filled her with confidence. Without second-guessing herself, she began to undo the buttons of his trousers. She pushed away the material and up sprung his shaft. It literally felt as if her eyes were bulging out of their sockets. She'd never seen such a thing before and it was glorious. Almost unable to help herself, she reached out until her fingers closed around his manhood. "Goodness, you feel so hard yet so smooth," she exclaimed.

It felt as if she was in a dream. A wickedly erotic dream that she didn't want to wake up from. Experimenting, she began to slide her hand up and down his phallus. It pulsed in response.

"That's it, my darling," Michael crooned to her. "Just like that."

He was growing harder with each and every stroke, and for a moment she became worried over how such a large thing was going to actually fit inside her. But she couldn't say anything to Michael, otherwise he would know she was a virgin and would insist they stopped. And she couldn't stop now. It was too delicious to stop.

"If you keep doing that," he said rather breathless. "I am not going to be able to prevent myself from spilling my seed."

"Oh." That was interesting.

Michael pulled her up toward him and flipped her over onto her back, swiftly pulling off her chemise, before he shimmied down to lay in between her thighs. He made quick work of removing her drawers and suddenly she was exposed to his gaze, which was feasting upon the sight of her nakedness. Holly thought she would have felt uncomfortable being naked in front of him, but the appreciation in his eyes filled her with such a sense of womanly confidence.

When Michael lowered his head and began to kiss the junction between her thighs, Holly nearly jumped from the bed. Never, had she felt such a thrill of pleasure as she did with his tongue and lips caressing her womanhood. Goodness, who would have thought such a thing was ever possible?

Unable to help herself, her hips started grinding up and down against his mouth as a pressure built deep inside of her. She clutched at the bedsheets by her side, gripping them tightly. Holly moaned aloud, unable to stop even if she tried.

It felt like she was reaching a peak, but she didn't know what was on the other side. She released the bedsheet and gripped his hair, almost urging him to suckle her more deeply, and then it was like a million stars burst all at once inside her as ripples of pleasure cascaded through her over and over again.

And just as she thought it couldn't get any better and thought it was over, he kept sucking on her, lapping up her juices until she started to orgasm again.

Then before she knew it, his cock replaced his mouth as he swiftly pushed himself inside her.

Her breath caught sharply in her throat. A searing pain tore through her as his shaft thrust through her maidenhead. Her inner passage felt like it was burning.

Michael paused, his shaft buried fully inside of her, beads of sweat dotting his brow. "You're a virgin?" There was such incredulity and a slight accusation in his voice as he tried to hold himself still above her.

"Please don't stop," she begged him, slowly moving her hips against his as the pain gradually started to recede. Though she wasn't experiencing the earth-shattering pleasure that his mouth had occasioned, having him inside of her, filling her completely, felt so right that she didn't want it to end.

"God," he moaned, seemingly unable to stop himself from starting to pump his shaft in and out of her passage. He reached a hand down between them and his thumb started to rub against the little nub of her womanhood.

The ripples of ecstasy started to build once again and her hips joined him thrust for thrust.

His mouth took her own in his as his chest pressed against her breasts. And then Holly felt the pleasure burst within her as she moaned over and over, before Michael groaned and pumped his seed inside her, until they were both spent.

They lay together, with Michael on top of her but slightly to her side, so as to not crush her, for what seemed like an age. She drifted off into a blissful sleep with the thought filling her mind that she was going to enjoy this particular part of their arrangement, greatly.

CHAPTER 8

THE SHAFT of light penetrating through the curtains was what woke her at first. But then when she saw Michael standing beside the window as still as a statue, silently staring out at the gardens below, her memories from the evening before came flooding back to her in full force, jolting away the remnants of sleep.

And oh, good lord, he was standing there naked too.

Holly gasped, glancing down at the bedsheet covering her. She was in Michael's bed and naked too. Mortification flooded her. She pulled the sheet up, ensuring every inch of her was covered, all the way to her chin. Her inhibitions had returned with full force in the light of day.

"Why didn't you tell me?" There was no warm morning greeting in his words as one might expect from a lover. Not that Holly really had any idea how a morning after was meant to be like, but she hadn't expected a coldly formal Michael. A man who was simply gazing out the window not even bothering to glance back at her. So distant and different to the gentle lover who'd held her last night and showed her what it was like to experience passion.

"Tell you what?" she asked, not liking the where the direction of this conversation was heading.

He straightened his shoulders, a rigidity within him she hadn't seen before.

"Tell me, that you were a virgin." His voice was monotone, and one would think he was discussing the weather, if not for the white of his knuckles as he clutched the frame of the window sill.

"Oh that." Embarrassment flooded her. Of course, she knew what he'd been referring to, she just hadn't wanted to address the issue. "I didn't think it was important."

"Not important?" Slowly he turned to face her. "Are you entirely serious? Of course, it was bloody important! I just took your virginity!"

"You don't have to yell," she pertly informed him.

"Was your husband so incompetent that he couldn't do the deed of actually making you his wife, or did you fabricate your poor dear Harold Carlton entirely?"

He was staring at her with such a look of accusation on his face, that for the first time she was scared. Not that he'd hurt her. Never of that. But she was scared that he would never forgive her for lying. And in that moment, she acknowledged that Michael was important to her. That he had always been since childhood, and their years apart had not changed her affections. She took in a deep breath and pulled her legs up to her chest, ensuring the sheet was still covering her fully. "I made him up."

For the space of a minute Michael said nothing, staring at her, his eyes wide with blame. "Of course, you did." He laughed bitterly. "Your housekeeper called you Miss Holly the other day when she was seeing me out, but I just thought it was a slip of the tongue. I should have known better. Especially taking into account your dowry. What man would turn away five-thousand pounds? None would. I was stupid to ever believe such a tale."

"You're certainly being stupid now carrying on like this." Holly raised her chin and met his gaze, only to be met with scorn.

"Oh, I am, am I?"

"Yes. Completely stupid!" she replied.

"Was it all a ruse then? To trap me?" There was an accusation in his gaze, but also what she thought could be hurt swirling underneath the anger too.

A slowly burning fury began to coil inside her belly. "Trap you with what?"

"With marriage, of course!"

"Marriage?" Her mouth dropped open. "What are you talking about? I don't want to marry you."

He stalked over to where his pants were laying on the floor and began shoving his feet through them. "No, of course you don't. Why would you wish to marry a viscount and heir to an Earldom, with buckets of money, estates and servants at his beck and call. Not when you can pretend to be a widow, living in a modest little town house instead."

"I adore my town house, thank you very much! I work extremely hard to afford the rent on it!" Holly pushed back the sheets, uncaring of her nudity as a mounting rage filled her. She marched over toward him. "And how dare you sit in judgment of me, when you have no clue what that stupid dowry of yours did."

Michael stopped buttoning his pants mid-button and gulped hard, seemingly unable to do anything else but stare at her. If she wasn't so furious she'd be somewhat satisfied that he seemed entranced by her body, but all it did now was make her mad. Mad that he'd ruined a perfectly good morning after one of the most amazing nights she'd ever had. "I didn't make up poor Harold to trick you into marriage,

Michael Drake!" she continued. "I made up poor Harold to protect myself and my sisters from my uncle, you dolt!"

She trudged over to where her chemise was laying on the floor and grabbed it, before tugging it over her head. "I wouldn't marry you if you begged me to. Not if you were the last man in England. Not if you were the last man on the entire planet. Not even for all the gold in the world. Why, not even if—"

"Alright, enough already!" he interrupted. "You've stated your position."

Holly glared at him as she pulled on her drawers, then her crinoline, tying it up at the back. "I hope so! Because honestly, as if I would marry England's answer to Don Juan! You're completely egotistical to think I orchestrated this all just to marry you. I had nothing to do with your stupid wager, now did I?"

"No," he conceded. "You didn't."

"You were the one pursuing me." She didn't even bother putting on her corset, instead she shoved her dress over her head, not even caring to tie up the ribbons at the back. "And yet you have the nerve to think I was trying to trap you into marriage!"

Holly didn't think she'd ever been so mad in her life. "You might be heir to an Earldom, Michael Drake, but you'd be a terrible husband!"

Michael hesitantly walked closer to where she was now trying to put on her cloak. "Why did you have to protect yourself?"

Suddenly, her anger evaporated and all she felt like doing was tucking herself into a ball and crying. She didn't want to tell him, but she knew she at least owed him an explanation for lying to him, even if he'd leaped to the ridiculous conclusion it was to trap him into marriage.

Taking in a deep breath she sank down to sit on the edge

of his bed. "After Edward died, our estate passed on to the next male heir which was my Uncle Reginald."

"A rather sniveling weasel, if I remember correctly." Michael gingerly sat down next to her.

"Yes, that perfectly describes him," she confirmed. "I often wondered how he and my father were brothers. They were the exact opposite of each other. My father was kind and generous and he loved to tinker with everything."

"Your father was a very good man and highly regarded," Michael agreed. "I missed him after he died. I especially missed our chats about his latest inventions, and being accepted by him, without any demands or expectations."

A sense of wistfulness filled her. There wasn't a day that she didn't miss her papa. He'd been the first to spark her interest with locks and anything mechanical, and though he was particularly absent minded when it came to the household, he'd had such a gift of imagination, that the house had always held such laughter and joy when he'd been around.

Things hadn't been the same since his death, and then when Edward was killed, her Uncle Reginald had showed up to claim his inheritance. "When my uncle found out about the dowry you'd bestowed on me, well one night, he and his son, my cousin Bernard convinced me to go to a county assembly with them both for a charity ball. Even though I was in mourning, it was for a very worthy cause so I agreed."

Taking in a deep breath, Holly's memories of that night rose to the surface. "It didn't take me long to realize that the carriage wasn't headed for the assembly."

"Where were they taking you?" Gently, Michael reached his hand across to cover hers.

The warmth of his skin touching her own was comforting. "To Gretna Green, apparently."

"What?" Michael all but roared. "The Devil they were!"

"My uncle wanted to get his hands on my dowry, you see, and had decided that I should marry Bernard for him to do so. He believed he was doing me a favor by kidnapping me. He said that if I married Bernard then my sisters and I would be allowed to stay in our home and he wouldn't throw us out into the streets."

"I'm going to kill the bastard." His grip on her hand tightened and Holly squeezed his hand back. "How did you get away?"

"I grabbed the lantern from inside the carriage and swung it into their thick heads. It knocked them out and I was able to get the carriage driver to stop the carriage. Then with the help of the pistol my uncle always kept under the seat in case of Highway robbers, I forced them all to the side of the road and took the carriage back home."

She glanced over to Michael and though there was anger burning brightly in his eyes, it wasn't directed at her any longer. "I knew I had to get my sisters out of there and quickly too, before my uncle and cousin eventually found a way to return. So, we packed up what little we could take with us and using the carriage fled to London."

"You should have come to me."

"You were fighting a war, Michael," she gently reminded him.

"How did you survive then?"

"Luckily, I had a very good friend living in London who was happy to hide us from my uncle until I could sort out what to do. And thankfully, the lock picking skills my father had taught me ended up being very useful."

"Oh God, you didn't resort to thievery, did you?"

Rather than be offended at the remark, Holly chuckled. "No, I did not resort to thievery. I discovered that my friend was being blackmailed. Someone had stolen her journal and was threatening to release the contents of it to Society, if she didn't keep paying him an income."

"And let me guess, you went and retrieved it for her, using your lock picking skills to do so?"

"Exactly so!" Holly enthused, relieved that she could finally tell someone the truth. "That was when my consultancy business was born."

"Your…consultancy business?" Michael sounded weary. "Why do I feel a headache coming on?"

"Word spread, anonymously of course, about my ability to successfully retrieve stolen items for ladies in precarious positions, and now I get paid a very healthy fee to do so. Enough so that I've been able to look after my sisters in comfort, if not luxury."

"And that's why you invented Harold. To lend an air of respectability to everything and protect your sisters and their reputations."

"Indeed, I did." She sighed. "My poor, wonderful, darling Harold, has been a life saver for me. I didn't want to kill him off, but a widow has so much more freedom. And being in mourning allowed myself and the girls to essentially stay hidden for a year, so that my uncle couldn't find us. And with Harold dead, I didn't have to make up any excuse surrounding a missing husband, instead I could extol on how amazing he had been. The perfect husband a girl could ever have."

"I imagine a pretend husband would be perfect," Michael muttered. "As he wouldn't talk back, or question you, or pull you into line. You'd have free reign with a husband like that."

"Yes, exactly. He was the most perfect of husband's, indeed." Holly turned to face Michael and smiled, but he was peering at her with such a look of intensity on his face that her smile disappeared.

"Well, I'm certainly not going to be perfect."

She blinked. Had she heard him correctly. "What are you saying, Michael?"

Letting go of her hand, he stood up abruptly and strode over to the door. "It means we're getting married, Holly. After I procure a special license."

"I'm not marrying you, Michael."

"You damn well are!" he said. "I promised your brother I would look after you, not that I would seduce and then abandon you."

"You didn't feel that way before you knew I was a virgin."

"And that very fact changes everything, completely. I have no intention of ruining you and then not making it right. I might be a bounder, but I'm not that much of a scoundrel."

"Well you haven't married any of your other conquests thus far, have you?"

"None of them were virgins." He dragged a hand through his thick hair and swore. "God damn it, Holly, you infuriate me at times."

And before she could respond further, he'd stalked back over to her, kissed her breathless and then strode out of the room without a backward glance.

For a minute, Holly sat there, speechless. He'd never bedded a virgin before? And he insisted on marrying her, now?

His upset was making a great deal more sense. But if the man thought he could simply dictate that they were getting married, he was quite mistaken, indeed. She had absolutely no intention of being shackled in matrimony to a rake who didn't love her. No, thank you very much! Especially, when he was only going to marry her to satisfy his idea of being noble and fulfilling his promise to her dying brother.

They'd be miserable in such a situation. Holly, the most miserable of all knowing he'd only married her out of a sense of duty and obligation which had nothing to do with love.

Particularly not, when she suspected she was starting to become a bit enamored with him. And caring for him, while watching him cavort with other women, which was something he was bound to eventually do, would rip her apart and destroy her.

Well, she wouldn't marry him. No matter how tempting the idea may be. She just had to stay strong against what she was sure would be a very determined viscount.

With her mind made up, she left his room, slipping though the hallways without being seen. He'd of course be furious she'd left, but best he realized sooner rather than later that she was an independent lady who would not be told what to do.

CHAPTER 9

MICHAEL STOOD pacing in her entrance hall, waving around the note she'd had delivered to him that afternoon, a massive scowl on his face, looking for all the world like a great big, angry bear.

"You refused to see me all day yesterday and now you summon me like some damned errand boy!" He stopped pacing and let out a harsh breath.

"Yes. I did," Holly answered, trying to hide the slight smile wanting to creep up the corners of her mouth. She imagined that the sight of Michael carrying on like he was would be enough to send most fleeing, but she thought it was rather adorable, and she'd missed him, having refused to see him all day yesterday after his declaration that they would be married. "Now, would you calm down so we can converse like rational adults."

"Calm down?" His eyes narrowed upon hers. "Calm down?" The timber of his voice ricocheted around the entrance, no doubt reaching every corner of her small townhouse and most likely into the neighbors' residence too.

"What is going on here?" Violet yelled as she skidded into

the hallway from the sitting room, her eyes darting between Holly and Michael in concern. "And why on earth are you roaring like a banshee, Lord Blackthorn?"

Holly couldn't help the bubble of laughter that rose out of her chest. She clapped a hand up to her mouth and tried to appear contrite, but if the expression on Michael's face was any indication, she was not being very successful in her endeavor. But comparing him to an Irish female spirit was rather hilarious.

"A banshee?" He spun around to face Violet, a thunderous expression on his face. "A banshee."

"Personally, I thought you sounded more like a bear," Holly pointed out.

Michael paused and seemingly tried to regain his patience, taking in a very deep breath and exhaling it, infinitely slowly. "You Jenkins' girls would try the patient of any man foolish enough to enter this residence."

"Doesn't say much about your state of mind, now does it?" Holly smiled sweetly at him. "For you are the one who entered."

"Holly!" Violet hissed. "What has gotten into you?"

She hadn't told Violet about her recently updated relationship status with the viscount, and she certainly hadn't mentioned that the blasted man had been demanding she marry him. After all, some things were best left in private, and besides there was no point in telling her sister about a marriage that was not going to eventuate. No matter how persistent Michael had been yesterday trying to discuss the matter with her.

If it hadn't been for Lord Pembrook's hunting party which was commencing later today, she would have refused to see Michael again until he agreed to cease and desist with his ridiculous demands that she marry him. Honestly, her plan to be his mistress was still perfectly acceptable even if he refused to now consider it.

The man had even had the nerve to go and procure the special marriage license he'd mentioned after finding out the truth of her widow status, or lack thereof. Why couldn't he simply be the rake society believed him to be? Things would be a great deal simpler for both of them if that was the case. Instead, he was acting all noble and honorable. Drat the man!

"I shall tell you what has got into her," Michael began, "the fact of the matter is your headstrong, stubborn, foolish sister, is refusing to marry me!"

Daphne, along with Mrs. O'Dowd, had chosen that moment to walk into the entrance hall too, and everyone except Holly and Michael gasped, with equal looks of absolute shock on all of their faces. It was almost like a pantomime. Holly sighed. Wonderful. Just wonderful.

"You've asked her to marry you?" Violet's eyes widened. "When did this happen?"

"Yesterday morning," Michael replied.

Holly cringed at the look of knowing now in her sister's face. There would be a great deal of questions from Violet when they were alone. Something else to look forward to, much like a tooth ache.

"And then, she refused to see me all of yesterday."

"Yes, we are quite aware of that fact," Daphne chimed in. "You did keep returning over and over yesterday."

"Much to all of our annoyance," Holly couldn't help but add.

"Well, once you agree to marry me I'll stop bothering everyone!" Michael replied.

"Marry you?" Holly exclaimed. "Why would I marry you? You haven't even asked me to marry you. You've simply demanded I do so."

"*Asked you?* You wouldn't bloody say yes, even if I did ask you to marry me. Would you!"

"That is beside the point. You've simply decided that we shall be married and have refused to listen to my opinion on the matter." She took several steps forward, over to where he was standing and couldn't help but poke him in the chest once again. "Of all the arrogant, presumptuous things, Michael Drake, that takes the cake!"

"Oh, it does, does it?" he growled.

She took a step back, flicking an imaginary speck of lint from her dress. "It most certainly does, and quite frankly, I have no wish to discuss the matter any further. I've made my position perfectly clear."

"As have I," there was a low warning tone in his voice. "And if you wish for me to take you to Pembrook's house party then you shall be going as my fiancée. And that is final."

Holly stomped her foot on the floor and clenched her fists. "You infuriating man. How dare you! We had a deal."

"A deal where you falsely represented yourself," he returned, but then he paused and looked around at their audience. "Do you really wish to discuss this here? I'm quite prepared to if you will not see reason."

"*Me*, see reason?" Oh, the nerve of the man. He infuriated her beyond belief. "You are the one being the stubborn blockhead about it all."

"A stubborn blockhead?" he all but spluttered.

"Children, children, children," Violet interrupted. "I hate to intrude on your rather amusingly immature quarrel, but you're—"

"Violet," Holly warned, "please stay out of it."

Violet regarded her with arched brow. "You're quarreling in the entrance hall, Holly. Hard to stay out of it in those circumstances. Perhaps you should discuss the matter in your study and give us all some peace."

Holly took in a rather ragged breath. Her sister had a point. But Michael made her so mad sometimes that she seemed to lose all reason. "You are quite right," she conceded. "The blockhead and I should finish our conversation in private." She motioned over to the doorway behind her.

Michael grunted, but nodded in agreement and followed her into her study. He kicked the door shut with his heel, just as Holly rounded on him. She'd been meaning to give him a piece of her mind, but instead found herself in his arms.

Pressing against him, their lips met in a fury of passion as they kissed each other until they were breathless. It was as if they couldn't get enough of each other. But then the kiss softened and the fury gave way to tenderness. A kiss as tantalizing as it was gentle. And oh, how she craved him more.

With a start, she realized how she'd missed him after having refused to see him all day yesterday, since he'd shown her the special license he'd obtained and demanded they go and get married then and there. Missed kissing him and being able to run her hands across the broad planes if his chest. Missed the very heat that radiated from him and warmed her as nothing else had in a long time.

It scared her how much she missed him, in truth.

Using all the willpower she possessed, she gently broke her lips free from his and pulled back from him. But she didn't have the willpower to pull back fully, instead staying in the circle of his arms and resting her head against his steady heartbeat. It took her a moment to settle her breathing back to a somewhat normal level.

Goodness the man held a physical pull over her, that was getting harder and harder to resist. With a sinking feeling, she knew her heart was in danger with this man as it never had been with another.

"So, what now?" His deep voice rumbled.

A very good question indeed. "I don't know." With great difficulty she pulled away from him and walked over to the front window. Glancing down into the street below, Holly was only vaguely aware of the passing carriages, and hackneys, all busily navigating the streets.

"Is marrying me, really such a horrible option?" he asked.

She glanced back over to him. There was an expression of boredom on his face, but Holly could see the slight stiffening of his jaw and knew that how she answered his question would be important for them both.

Taking in a deep breath, she shook her head. "No, of course not."

"Then I don't understand the problem." He strode over to where she stood and took her hands in his own. "You will eventually be a countess Holly and will never want for anything in your life. Your sisters will be looked after and under my protection. They will have their pick for a husband."

"Why are you so insistent on marriage, Michael?" She all but pleaded with him. "You're meant to be one of the most infamous rakes in England. Why would you want to get married?"

"I promised your brother I would look after you."

"You can still do that if I'm your mistress."

"Damn it, Holly!" He snapped, releasing her hands abruptly. "I took your virginity. That means something to me and it should to you too."

"But what about love, Michael?"

His face seemed to blanch of color. "What about it?"

"Call me old fashioned, but I always dreamt that one day when I did marry, I would be marrying the love of my life. That I would have a marriage like my parents. Which is something that you can't give me, is it?"

"You're not some green chit, fresh out of the nursery,

Holly," Michael replied, his voice oddly devoid of emotion. "You know that marriages within society are business transactions. Nothing more, nothing less."

"Of course, I know that," she responded. "But not all of them are. And I certainly don't mean to have such a marriage. In fact, at my age I thought marriage was quite off the cards. And to be quite honest, Michael, I'd rather stay a spinster for the rest of my life than live in a loveless marriage."

He gave a mirthless laugh. "You're being foolishly naïve."

"Perhaps," she conceded. "But why is it you're so afraid of love?"

A muscle in his jaw twitched. "Damn it, just leave it alone. There are things I've done that you would hate me for."

"Such as what?"

For a moment, she thought he was going to tell her but then he shook his head.

"Things that happened in the Crimea that I don't wish to go into." His expression was completely aloof.

"Very well. That is your choice," she conceded. "But I know I'd rather be happy on my own, than unhappy in a loveless marriage."

"You certainly know how to crush a man's ego, don't you?" He sighed, long and loudly. "And what about children? Have you even considered that aspect of it?"

"What do you mean, children?" she asked, unable to suppress the image of herself cradling a child in her arms who had the same blue eyes and brown hair as Michael. The very image awoke a yearning inside her she hadn't known she'd possessed.

"I know you were a virgin," he began. "But surely even being a virgin you are aware that after the other night you could potentially be carrying my child within your womb."

Holly gulped. "Oh. I hadn't considered that aspect of it."

"No, I'd gathered not." He stared over her head and out the window. "I will not have a child of mine growing up a bastard."

"Well there is no need to be so crass about it."

"It's simply a fact, Holly." Michael glanced back down at her. "And I'm sure you wouldn't want your child to be born with such a stigma either."

"No," she conceded. "The world is a harsh enough place as it is."

"Perhaps then I can offer a compromise?"

Holly pursed her lips. "Do you even actually know what the word compromise means, Michael?"

"Holly," his deep voice rumbled. "I'm being serious."

"So was I." She sighed. "Oh, very well, I'm listening. What is this compromise you wish to suggest?"

"Obviously, you don't think I'd make you a good husband—"

"I never said that, though that's probably a part of it," she interrupted him. "However, what I said was I didn't wish to be married without love."

"But do you at least agree with me that you don't know, not positively, until you try it?"

"What? Do you mean live in a loveless marriage?"

He nodded. "Perhaps it might not have love, but it would have mutual respect."

She had no idea where he was going with this line of thought, but she was curious enough to play along, for the moment. "I suppose that could be the case."

"Though we have argued over the years and still continue to do so on occasion," he said. "I like you Holly. I really like you. I always have."

A feeling of happiness filled her. "I like you too." And she did, even if they did disagree on a great deal of things.

"We understand each other," he continued, "and though I

know I could never give my heart to you. To anyone, for that matter, I believe we can make a marriage together work. I believe that mutual respect is far more important than any supposed feelings of love, which is simply lust in disguise and fleeting at that."

"You really do have a poor opinion of love, don't you?" She found herself extremely curious to know how he'd gotten so jaded about the subject and what he'd done that he thought she'd hate him for. "What exactly is it that you are proposing?"

"I shan't insist we get married straightaway."

"My, how very gracious of you." She hoped the sarcasm in her voice penetrate that rather thick head of his.

He breathed out a long breath. "Instead, we shall announce our engagement."

"Our engagement?" She pinched the bridge of her nose, not liking this plan of his already.

"Yes," he confirmed. "You will agree to be my betrothed, which will lend a level of respectability to us being constantly seen together and then if you still don't wish to marry me and decide you've had enough of our affair, you can cry off painting me as the villainous fiancé, which my reputation will assist in. Then you shall be able to continue to play the widow and maintain your respectability."

"So, you won't continue to attempt to force me to marry you?" She couldn't shake the feeling that there was something she was missing about this whole deal.

"Provided you're not pregnant and that you keep an open mind about actually marrying me, then no, I won't."

"And if I am with child?"

"Am I really so bad of a prospect if you are?" She could hear the hurt in his voice that he tried to disguise.

"No, of course you're not." And truly he wasn't. "Does that mean we must stop being intimate with each other to avoid an accidental pregnancy? If that is the case it rather defeats one of the main purposes of my plan, to experience pleasure before I'm too old. Although I must admit too that I never thought of the possibility of pregnancy, which I probably should have."

"There are ways to prevent pregnancy and still be intimate," Michael said, looking none too pleased to be discussing such a topic. "But they're not foolproof, though are generally effective."

Holly was intrigued. "Well that is good then. We shall have to employ them."

"Or you could just marry me and we wouldn't have to worry."

She narrowed her eyes. "You were in the midst of compromising, remember?" Goodness most people would think she was mad if they knew she hadn't said yes to marrying him, immediately. Perhaps she was mad? After all, what woman wouldn't want to be a countess, surrounded by wealth and luxury?

But none of that mattered, not when Holly thought about potentially being married to him and stupidly unable to resist giving him her heart, while he couldn't reciprocate her feelings. And without love, what was to stop him from having mistresses and breaking her heart every time she found out about one of them? Nothing, is what.

That would be torturous. Absolutely torturous. She would have to guard her heart fiercely as she rather suspected it was well on the way to already being rather enamored of the man. "Very well," she finally agreed. "I shall pretend to be your fiancée for as long as we decide our affair should last, but when I do cry off you will agree not to force a marriage between us. Oh, and that you also take me to Lord Pembrook's this afternoon."

"Ah yes, the reason for my summons today. How could I

forget?" This time it was he who had sarcasm dripping from his words.

"Well I hope you took heed of the note I sent you and came packed, with your carriage ready to go." Holly sailed past him toward the door. "It is a good four-hour ride to his estate is it not? I would like to get there when the others do. Showing up with you, will already create a spectacle, which can hopefully be minimized by at least arriving on time."

"Good Lord, you're tenacious when you've decided upon something aren't you?"

She paused with a hand on the door handle, jiggling it a bit to give her sisters, who were surely pressed up against the wood of the door trying to eavesdrop, time to move away from it. "I certainly am, Michael Drake, and I think you'd do well to remember that. Now, shall we be off? As I said, I don't wish to be late."

CHAPTER 10

"CONSIDERING we're not far from Pembrook's estate, don't you think it's perhaps time you explain to me why you're searching his safes?" Michael asked, trying to stretch his legs out in the small confines of the carriage, with little success. He'd been cooped up in the cramped space for nearly four hours and not only was the lack of room starting to grate on his nerves, but he'd spent the better part of the trip restraining himself from grabbing Holly and hauling her onto his lap.

Wanting to do so, was like a compulsive reflex that kept battering his will. But he couldn't give in to temptation. The woman was as clever as a whip and if she knew that all he could think about was caressing her and being inside her, filling her once again with his seed, she'd use that power to manipulate him. All women did, why should Holly be different? Plus, he had a feeling that he'd need to keep his wits about him this weekend. Especially if she was going to be sneaking off to crack Pembrook's safe at some point.

He still couldn't even believe that he was a party to such a thing. After the war had ended he'd hoped his days of cloak-

and-dagger activities would be well and truly behind him. Not so with Holly Jenkins it seemed.

"I've told you," the lady herself spoke up from where she was seated across from him on the blue velvet seat of his carriage, the purple skirts of her traveling gown spread across the entire width of the bench. "Pembrook has some incriminating letters belonging to my friend, which I must retrieve." She shrugged, her eyes glued to the window and the passing scenery. "I can't reveal anything else, without risking a confidence."

"And you know for certain it is Pembrook blackmailing this woman?"

Holly nodded. "Yes, quite certain."

It was somewhat surprising, given that he'd always considered Pembrook a weak fool and blackmailing someone usually took nerves of steel. Though the man had recently suffered some financial setbacks. "I had heard he'd made some terrible investments of late." Michael shrugged. "Perhaps that's why he's felt the need to dabble in blackmail."

"It would make sense," Holly agreed. "Though I intend to put a stop to his nefarious activities once I find the letters." She turned to face him, and Michael was struck by how darned gorgeous she was. Her almond eyes were gleaming a brilliant emerald in the afternoon sunlight and her ebony hair was swept up high on her head, with her bonnet covering most of the luscious locks, but with a few curls cascading down, framing her heart shaped face. "Michael?" she asked, with a slight hesitation in her voice that was unusual for Holly.

"Yes?"

"This new agreement we've struck...well, I do hope it involves...um..." She blinked her eyes closed and took in a deep breath. "More of what we did at your house, the other evening."

A jolt of lust gripped him, all but consuming in its intensity. Caring little about his earlier worries, Michael reached over and plucked her up from her seat, pulling her onto his lap, crinoline and all.

She laughed and grabbed his shoulders. It was one of the sweetest sounds he'd heard. God, this woman did things to him. Frustrated him to no end one moment and then had him burning with desire the next. No woman had ever affected him like Holly Jenkins did. It would be very easy to imagine her in his life always. Like a bright light shining warmth and happiness into his lonely and dark existence.

He already felt happier with her in these last few days, than he had been in the past several years. And seeing her smile and hearing her laughter was becoming the most favorite part of his day.

A voice in his head whispered he should be scared, but it was quickly quashed when Holly wriggled her derrière on his lap, the crinoline of her skirt making it somewhat difficult in the small space, but neither of them caring. "I haven't been able to stop thinking about you," Michael whispered against her lips as his hands circled around her waist, wishing that there was nothing between his skin and hers.

Her whole face lit up with his confession. "You haven't?"

"No. I haven't," he admitted, beginning to rain kisses down the column of her neck. He could smell the rose scent of her again and breathed it in deeply. Roses had never smelt as good as they did on Holly. "Images of you naked in my bed, have been on my mind, constantly."

"I must admit, I haven't been able to think of much else, either," Holly replied, wiggling her backside against him and smiling, as his shaft stood to attention, straining against the material of his trousers and begging to be released.

Michael groaned and his head swooped down to capture

her lips in his own, kissing her until they were both panting in need. "God, you taste delicious," he murmured in-between kisses. "So desirable and sweet, I can't get enough."

"I've missed your kisses." She was breathing hard, her face flushed and her eyes alight with excitement.

He chuckled. "I only kissed you a few hours ago."

She wound her arms around his neck. "I meant, yesterday after I left your house. I didn't get to kiss you for a full twenty-four-hours."

"And whose fault was that, hmm?" he rumbled against her ear as his hand slowly circled around the material covering her breast. "I did all I could to speak with you yesterday, but you refused to see me."

Holly pulled back from him slightly. "That's because you were waving around a special license for marriage. Not the way to sweep a lady off her feet, let me assure you."

"Probably not," he agreed. "Can I tell you something? As much as you've infuriated and challenged me over these last few days, I don't think I've ever been quite so happy."

A gorgeous smile lit up her face once again. "You make me happy too. And I certainly can't wait to feel you inside of me again."

Michael groaned at the thought, but before he could reply, the carriage started slowing. He glanced out the window and swore softy as Pembrook's manner came into view. "We're going to have to continue this later tonight, my dear."

"We're here already?" Her eyes went round as she scrambled from his lap, across to the other seat and quickly straightened out her skirts. She then reached up and tucked away some stray strands of hair that had escaped her bonnet and took in a few steadying breaths. "How do I look? Presentable I hope?"

She looked bloody gorgeous, but with a frown of

annoyance, he realized that all the other men there would think that too.

"What? Is something wrong with my appearance?"

Michael shook his head. "You look fine. Too damned good, in fact." He couldn't be certain, but it looked like her lips twisted up at the corner a fraction.

The carriage came to a halt and there waiting for them, were Lord and Lady Pembrook.

"Welcome to Pembrook Manor, Blackthorn," Pembrook's voice boomed out a greeting as he walked over to the carriage door, now being held open by one of his footmen. "And my dear Mrs. Carlton, I'd heard you would be joining us as Blackthorn's guest. A big welcome indeed!"

Holly took the man's extended hand and stepped down onto the gravel of the path. "My thanks, my Lord. I do hope that won't be any trouble?"

"Of course not," the man assured her as he guided her over to his wife. Michael followed behind them watching as Holly greeted the lady of the house. He in turn then shook Pembrook's hand and kissed Lady Pembrook's gloved knuckles.

As Holly and Lady Pembrook walked ahead of them, happily chatting away together, Pembrook and he walked alongside each other.

"We have two *adjoining* rooms prepared for you both." Pembrook angled his face around and winked at Michael, a large grin plastered over his florid fleshy complexion. "I do hope that will suit?"

Michael nodded and raised his brow when Pembrook leaned in bit closer to him so only the two of them could hear.

"I must say," Pembrook whispered, "I was very curious to know who you were with in my study the other night and then when I received your note asking if Mrs. Carlton could attend with you, well then, let us just say the mystery was solved!"

"How clever of you," Michael began. "Obviously, your powers of deduction are...*astounding*."

The man beamed, his smile spread practically from ear to ear. "Yes, well, I have a good nose for things, to be sure."

"To be sure," Michael agreed. Clearly, the sarcasm had been lost on the man.

"And I hope you don't mind, but after I received your note I went to White's and put some money on you winning the Mistletoe Mistress bet!" The man laughed. "Nothing like a bit of inside information, don't you agree? I put down one hundred pounds that you would be the one to successfully woo Mrs. Carlton and make her your mistress."

Michael wasn't surprised that the wager had become common knowledge at Whites. Generally, most wagers did, resulting in a great many side bets being made by the other members of the club too. Though he didn't like how cavalier Pembrook was being about the matter. "Your money is lost, I'm afraid."

Pembrook faltered in his step. "I beg your pardon?"

"You heard me well enough." Michael continued to stride ahead, with Pembrook scrambling to catch up. "And if you continue to disrespect my fiancée by suggesting she is my Mistletoe Mistress, then you shall find yourself having to name your seconds."

There was a look of perplexed shock on the man's face. "The two of you are engaged?"

It was Michael's turn to stop. Pembrook followed suit.

"Do you need your ears checked, man?" Michael asked. "Mrs. Carlton has done me the honor of agreeing to be my fiancée, not my mistress. So, if you continue to call her my mistress, I shall take offense and will have to satisfy such a thing by challenging you to a duel. Can I be any plainer?"

It took a few seconds for the man to react, but he hastily gulped and nodded. "No, no need. I understand you perfectly." The man's eyes lit up in wild speculation "Apologies if you thought I was being disrespectful! I meant no offense and indeed I would say congratulations are in order!"

He took Michael's hand and shook it again, heartily.

"You'll also be very glad to know," Pembrook continued. "That the Devil Duke and St Giles are here. They were most pleased to learn that Mrs. Carlton would be a guest of mine too. I might have hinted that you'd be sharing some news with them soon." He rubbed his hands together in glee. "Must admit, I'm rather looking forward to the looks of shock and surprise that shall grace their faces when they realize they've lost the bet to you. Jolly good fun!"

The fact that Michael had slept with Holly and made her his, still didn't lessen his annoyance over his two friends being there. He hadn't liked how either of them had looked at Holly and though he knew they wouldn't attempt to seduce her once they found out Michael was engaged to her, they had still been contemplating seducing her for their stupid bet.

After all, who wouldn't want Holly to be theirs. She was smart, charming, and absolutely stunning. She cared about others, more than she did herself. She was funny and her very touch excited him more than any other woman's ever had. With all of those qualities, of course those two bounders would be interested in her. And if she did break off their engagement as she said she intended, then those two wouldn't be able to help themselves from pursuing her, rakes that they were.

Well. Not on his watch they wouldn't!

Michael would simply have to make sure that she didn't end their engagement. Whatever it took.

CHAPTER 11

SOME FORTY MINUTES LATER, after both Holly and Michael had been shown to their respective rooms, Holly made her way downstairs to the back veranda where afternoon tea was being served.

There were about twenty people already milling around the space, nibbling on pastries and cake, with laughter and chatter abounding. She didn't need to scan her eyes across the space to know that Michael hadn't yet made his way downstairs. Of late, every time he was within her vicinity a prickle of awareness would dance along the nape of her neck, warning her that he was near.

And sadly, that prickle of awareness was absent at the moment.

Holly sighed, before winding her way around the various huddles of guests, toward where Lady Pembrook was standing in the far corner talking with a gentleman.

As Holly got closer however, she saw it wasn't just any gentleman the woman was talking to, it was Devlin Markham, the Duke of Huntington. Her eyes narrowed as they landed on the man's own. He grinned at her and had the audacity to wink. The very gesture causing many sighs from the other ladies in the vicinity. Holly had to refrain from rolling her eyes. The man was certainly handsome, and aside from Michael, he probably was the handsomest man she had in fact seen, though he didn't affect her like Michael did, which thankfully meant she was immune to the Devil Duke's charms.

The man broke away from his conversation with Lady Pembrook and strode over toward Holly.

"Why Mrs. Carlton, fancy seeing you here?" the duke said, bowing over her hand and kissing the back of her knuckles. "Blackthorn didn't accompany you downstairs?"

Holly's mouth fell open. "How did you know I was here with him?"

The duke shrugged. "I have my sources. Not to mention Lord Pembrook couldn't wait to tell me when I arrived."

He grinned at her and Holly couldn't help but grin back.

"I imagine the man took great joy in telling you such a thing," she replied.

The duke nodded. "He did, to be sure. So, it is true, you're here with Blackthorn." It was a statement, not a question.

"I'm afraid you will not win you wager, Your Grace." Holly was very satisfied when the first hint of surprise widened the corners of his eyes. She imagined he wasn't a man that was surprised very often, if at all.

"You know of the wager?" he asked.

"I do. In fact, I think most people in society do by now," she replied. "Oh, and I can comfortably confirm that I am Lord Blackthorn's mistletoe mistress."

His lips drew up at the corners of his mouth, in a smile instead of the frown she had been expecting to see. "Well, I'm very glad to hear it."

Another response she certainly hadn't been expecting. "You are?"

"Yes," he confirmed. "The amount of times that Michael has mentioned you over the years, without even realizing it, well I knew he needed somewhat of a push in the right direction."

"Excuse me?" Now it was Holly's turn to be surprised. "You were playing matchmaker?"

"I'm not as much of a blackguard as most seem to believe." The duke shrugged. "When we were upstairs at Pembrook's and I saw you outside through the window and that you were about to be the next lady through the entrance, I came up with the idea for the wager."

Astonishment almost stole her breath. "Who comes up with such a wager on the spot?"

"Clearly someone who is very bored, though wants to see his friend happy." Huntington shrugged. "Blackthorn's been different after the war. Lonely even. I just wished to see him happy and thought the wager might do it."

Holly was certain that her jaw was now hanging on the ground. "You didn't..."

"Sometimes it's a friend's job to push another friend in the right direction, my dear Mrs. Carlton." He reached out and took her hand in his once again. "But perhaps let us keep that as our secret. Shall we?"

Holly felt the funny prickle along her neck, a moment before Michael's roar echoed behind her.

"Secret?" Michael yelled. "What bloody secret?"

Everyone around them stopped talking as they all turned to look at the three of them. Holly felt the heat of embarrassment rush up her cheeks. She was not at all used to being the center of attention as obviously the two knuckle heads next to her were. She didn't like it at all.

"Ah, you've finally decided to join us, have you?" The duke clearly wasn't at all intimidated by Michael's outburst. He was a far braver man than most.

"You're not bloody doing anything with her, let alone keeping secrets!" Michael stalked over to the duke until he was standing only a few inches away. "She is my fiancée. Do you understand, me? Mine."

A muscle in Holly's jaw began to twitch. "I am not yours. I'm not any man's, for that matter. And how dare you announce such a thing for all the world to hear!" She swept her arm wide to encompass the crowd still gathered about, pretending not to listen to their conversation, but failing miserably. There wasn't a single ear not angled toward them, and what was worse, the story would spread like wildfire once they all returned to London on Monday.

Michael scoffed. "I would hardly call Pembrook's back veranda and the people within it, the world."

Her anger began to boil to the surface. "I was not being literal, you blockhead!"

"That is the third time you've called me that today," Michael's voice was a low growl as he turned to face her. "Don't do it again."

"Don't you dare tell me what to do, Michael Drake!" Holly's voice was vibrating with fury. "I shall call you a blockhead when your behavior clearly warrants such a term. Though perhaps there are better terms for you. What about a bell swagger then? Or a bottle head even?" She crossed her arms over her chest. "Either of those two would be perfect descriptions of you."

Behind him the duke started laughing.

Michael narrowed his eyes. "I don't even know what those names mean!"

"Oh, allow me to assist," the duke happily answered. "A bottle head means someone devoid of wit, and a bell swagger, if I'm not mistaken, means a noisy bullying fellow. Is that quite right, Mrs. Carlton?"

"Quite correct, Your Grace," Holly answered him. "Apt descriptions for Lord Blackthorn, do you not agree?"

"Perfect, actually," the duke replied. "Particularly the bell swagger one. 'Tis much closer to the truth."

Michael scowled at them. "Stop it, both of you."

"Or what?" Holly rounded on him. "You shall end our *betrothal*? Well, you have no need to worry, because I've decided to end things with you, right now! I have no time or patience to deal with a man throwing a tantrum and I certainly shall not stay engaged to one!" *Even if it was a temporary engagement.* She swiveled on her heel and marched past the crowd of gawkers, her boots clicking over the tiles in a furious march.

How dare the man try to dictate to her, even if she had been calling him names. Why the very nerve of him, daring to try to tell her what she could or could not do or say, was simply infuriating! Honestly, he deserved to be called every name under the sun.

CHAPTER 12

Holly paid little heed to her surroundings as she stalked through the corridor toward the main staircase which would take her to her room; too annoyed over her encounter with Michael to think about anything else. The man simply infuriated her with his bossy ways. He always had. Probably why they'd regularly clashed over the years.

But everything was different now. Their entire relationship was different. And if the man thought for a minute that just because they had become intimate she would put up with being dictated to, he was sorely mistaken. Goodness, she could only imagine how much more autocratic he would be if they were married.

Not that she wanted to marry him. *Liar.* A voice whispered in her head. Damned annoying voice!

Well of course she'd imagined what it would be like to be married to him. What woman wouldn't? She'd be the Viscountess of Blackthorn, and with Michael as her husband, her uncle wouldn't ever be able to threaten them again.

Holly stopped short when she passed Pembrook's study. Taking a few steps backward she glanced around the hallway.

Not a soul around. Most of the guests and Pembrook's servants were all occupied with the afternoon tea being served on the terrace.

Casually, she took a few steps over toward his study and peered into the room. It was empty.

This could be the perfect time to search his safe, and if she was successful then she could go home and leave the blockhead here.

Stepping into the study Holly's gaze skimmed across the inside of the room. It was predominantly decorated with rich walnut and deep navy-blue colors, and there was a large desk on the right side of the room with several book shelves surrounding the exterior of the room, and a green velvet settee and armchairs were on the left side. There was also a large picture frame containing a portrait of Pembrook and his wife above the mantle behind his desk. A perfect place to hide a safe.

Gathering her courage Holly stepped into the room, gently closing the door behind her. Hopefully, she would hear the door opening, which would give her time to mask what she was really doing. Before she could think better of it, she strode over to the desk and walked behind it to where the picture was hanging on the wall. Lord and Lady Pembrook were staring down at her from the portrait, both with rather severe expressions painted on their faces, though Holly suspected the artist had been rather generous with his brush. They looked far more striking in the portrait than in person.

She reached her fingers up to the gold gilt frame and gently began feeling around its edges. Her fingers brushed along a little knob. She pressed it. A distinct click sounded, and the left side of the portrait popped open toward her. Success! Holly swung open the portrait fully, noting the hinges hidden on the right-hand side along the inside of the frame.

And there before her, sitting gloriously in the wall, was a classic Chubb safe. A rather old model that Pembrook should have had updated years ago if he was serious about protecting anything inside. It was one of the first safes Holly had learned how to pick, in an effort to assist her father in developing a more robust locking mechanism, that was nigh in impossible to crack. And he'd come close to developing one, before he'd died.

The familiar squeeze of pain whenever she thought about her father, tightened around her heart. She still missed him dreadfully and the times spent tinkering together picking locks and safes in his workshop, were some of her most treasured memories. Except for the last memory, when together in his workshop they had finally cracked a supposedly uncrackable safe and they'd both being dancing around in joy, when suddenly he'd clutched his chest and collapsed onto the ground, not breathing. And Holly hadn't been able to save him.

The doctor had said it was an episode of his heart and that there was nothing anyone could have done, but a part of her had always felt responsible and guilty for not being able to do more.

Then shortly after, her brother had gone off to fight in the Crimea with Michael. But even before he could get to the battlefront, he'd died a pointless death in a drunken fight. The very thought of the futility of his death brought with it the usual sense of anger and frustration. For him to be taken from them, after they'd only recently lost their father, was cruel beyond measure. A need to ask Michael exactly what had happened rose within her, but as with the many times before, fear of not wanting to delve too deeply into the matter suppressed the desire.

Shaking the memories away, Holly knew she had to concentrate on her task at hand. She couldn't get caught trying to get inside Pembrook safe as such a thing would bring with it dire consequences, and if something happened to her, who would look after her sisters? Michael's dowry would only make them targets for fortune hunters. Reaching into the pocket of her dress, Holly pulled out her trusty set of lock-picks, which she always carried with her.

Quickly, she got to work, softly cooing to the lock as she manipulated it with her picks. Within about a minute the sound of the pin-tumblers falling into place was like music to her ears. A delightful melody, that she never tired of. She twisted her pins and the door to the safe unlatched and opened. "Thank you, my darling!" she whispered to the lock, knowing most would think her crazy for doing so, but it had become somewhat of a routine, after all.

She pulled the door of the safe wide open and jackpot! Well at least she hoped so. Unlike the safe at Pembrook's townhouse, this one actually had papers inside it, and she prayed that Lady Clare's letters were amongst them. She reached out and grabbed them all, quickly rifling through them. A moment later she found what she'd come for. Thank the Lord.

It was the two letters Clare had begged her to retrieve. Two letters, that would ruin the lady's marriage if the truth ever came out. Stuffing them into her pocket, Holly was about to replace the other correspondence back into the safe, when she noticed the names of several prominent ladies and gentlemen scrawled on the papers.

Her eyes skimmed over the letters and she quickly realized that Lady Clare wasn't the only one Pembrook may have been blackmailing. All of the documents were either letters or notes outlining various historical events that if released, would cause great embarrassment and scandal to those names written upon the sheets.

Her heart fell when Michael's name appeared. Not that she should be surprised, he was an extremely well-known libertine. But Pembrook was a fool to think of blackmailing him. Michael would never heed any sort of demands for payment, instead he'd rip the man to shreds.

Did she dare read what sort of scandal he'd been involved in? She didn't think she could, but then, she gasped when she read Edward's name too. Edward had never been involved in any scandal. Had he?

She took in a deep lungful of air and began reading. With each word, her heartache grew.

If what she was reading was correct, Edward hadn't died in simply a tavern fight as they'd all been led to believe, but he'd died saving Michael.

A heaviness settled deep in her stomach. Michael had been responsible for Edward's death? No, surely that wasn't right. If he had been, he would have said something. He couldn't think to be intimate with her, marry her even, without telling her such a thing...could he?

There had to be a mistake. Once she spoke to him about the matter, he'd surely confirm it was an error. That he hadn't been the cause of her brother's death.

Quickly, she stuffed all of the papers into the two pockets of the skirts of her dress, then retrieved her picks from the lock, before closing the safe and then the picture frame.

For a moment after, she simply stood there, with her hands up on either side of the frame, leaning against it, thoughts of Michael spinning around in her head. He would tell her it was false. He had to.

The very distinct sound of the hammer of a pistol being cocked brought Holly back to the reality of her situation with a jolt, and she spun around to face the threat.

Fear gripped her when she saw her uncle standing there, pistol in his hand and pointed directly at her. Lady Pembrook was standing next to him, in front of what had been a portion of the bookcase, but which was now swinging wide open with a dark passageway behind it. A secret passageway. No wonder she hadn't heard any noises to alert her to the danger.

"Hello my dear niece." Her uncle's pinched voice was about as welcoming as the sound of nails scraping over the surface of a blackboard. "How wonderful it is to have finally found you. I've been searching for quite some time, you see."

"And looks like we've caught her in time before she could get into the safe," Lady Pembrook remarked, her voice even and steady, almost as if she were discussing the weather.

"What are you doing here, uncle?" Holly asked, her eyes scanning across the room for an exit. She could possibly make a run for the door, but by the time she wrenched it open he could shoot her. But would he? Surely he wouldn't dare risk such a thing? But then again if no one knew he was here, he could easily do so and then flee back down the passageway, with none being the wiser. Except for Lady Pembrook. "And Lady Pembrook, why are you helping him?"

The lady shrugged. "I don't know if you're aware of it, but Lord Pembrook has got the estate into a bit of a financial bind."

"Is that why he's trying to blackmail Lady Clare?" It would make sense.

"*My* husband, try to blackmail someone?" Lady Pembrook burst out laughing. "Oh, how hilarious. My husband is a complete buffoon, who has neither the vision nor the courage to do any such thing. No, it was I who was blackmailing Lady Clare." She strolled over to the door of the study and twisted the lock.

Holly's hopes fell. That had been her only way out, apart from the secret passage behind her uncle.

"Obviously, I cannot have you interfering in my very lucrative endeavors," Lady Pembrook announced. "Which is why I contacted your uncle and alerted him to your whereabouts."

"But how did you know I was searching for the incriminating letters?" Holly asked her.

The woman shrugged. "When my husband mentioned he'd found Lord Blackthorn and a lady in his study on the night of our ball, I knew straight away something was amiss as Blackthorn is far too sophisticated to bother with such nonsense in someone else's study, instead of his own bed. Considering my little hobby, I thought I may have been found out and perhaps he and whoever the lady he was with were actually searching for any evidence of my blackmail."

"Well you certainly have been discovered now," Holly pointed out, knowing that she needed to get out of this room, and now. Perhaps if she ran at her uncle, she could topple him over? She doubted Lady Pembrook would lower herself to wrestling her, if her uncle was knocked out.

"Only by you my dear," Lady Pembrook pointed out. "In any event, as soon as I found out you were the lady Blackthorn was chasing, I did some digging and discovered your maiden name and your details. Which is how I alerted your uncle to the situation." With a sweep of her hand, Lady Pembrook motioned to the passageway. "Feel free to take her, Sir Reginald, for she is all yours."

"Come along then, Holly," he said, with such a look of satisfaction in his gaze that Holly felt like stalking up to him and punching him in the nose. Something she probably would have done, if he hadn't been aiming a pistol at her. "It is time for you to properly be married, rather than pretending you were."

"If you think I shall meekly go with you, you've clearly forgotten our last encounter, uncle," she reminded him.

The man's face twisted into a cruel smiled. "Oh, I haven't forgotten, my dear niece. In fact—" he pulled back some greying brown hair from his forehead, "—I still have the scar to remind me."

A thin white line, over an inch long, stretch along his forehead, just below his hairline. The remnants from having swung the carriage lantern at the man's head on their last meeting, Holly supposed. Good. She was glad it had left a mark. It was the least he deserved. "I'm surprised you're trying again then," Holly responded. "One would think; you might have learned your lesson that I do not take well to being kidnapped!"

His whole body seemed to clench tightly in anger. "You will do as you're told, for once in your life, girl, or you shall feel a bullet in your stomach! My brother let you all run ragged. Fancy allowing you to work on his gadgets and pick locks. Why, it simply isn't done! No wonder you've turned into such a headstrong, recalcitrant female!"

"Why thank you, uncle. I think that may be the very first compliment you've ever paid me." Holly smiled over at him, hoping such a gesture would agitate him enough that it might give her an opportunity to flee.

"Shut up, you stupid girl," he growled, using the shaft of the weapon to motion her toward the passageway. "Once you belong to Bernard, I am going to take great pleasure in showing him exactly how to punish you properly with a bloody good beating! Now, unless you want to be shot, I suggest you start walking."

Holly had never been prone to panicking, but her palms were starting to get clammy, and her throat felt as dry as sand-paper. Without the smallest doubt, she knew she couldn't go down that passageway. "What do you actually intend to do?" If she could get him talking, maybe she could think of some way to get out of this mess. "I will never agree to marry Bernard."

"Then I shall have to kill you," he purred as he walked across to her, stopping barely a foot away.

"I think death would be preferable to having you as my father-in-law."

He slapped her hard across her cheek, and Holly nearly fell over, stumbling to her side and toward the wall, her ears ringing and her cheek stinging like it was aflame.

"If I die you won't get my dowry."

"No," he agreed. "But one of your sisters will do equally as well. Perhaps even the youngest one will be more biddable than you."

She blinked for a moment, slowly regaining her footing as his words penetrated into her awareness. Glancing across at him, Holly saw he had a tight smile on his face, but there was such cunning blazing in his eyes that suddenly she knew that was his plan all along. With her out of the way, it would be much easier to kidnap Daphne who was only seventeen.

A burning rage unlike anything Holly had ever felt, consumed her. Without thought, she lunged at him.

They began to wrestle before the pistol roared, deafeningly, around the room.

CHAPTER 13

"I WOULD LEAVE HER BE, my friend," Huntington's hand gripped around Michael's arm.

Michael wrenched away from Devlin's grip and twisted around to confront the man, his lips drawn back in a snarl. "Friend? You dare to call yourself my friend, when you're trying to keep secrets with my...my...well with Holly? Were you planning to seduce her and think to keep it a secret from me?"

There was neither anger or upset on Huntington's seemingly implacable face. "Don't be a fool, Michael. You know I wouldn't do anything of the sort."

"Do I? Do I really?" Michael felt the frustration roll over him in waves. A part of him knew he could trust Huntington, even if no one else in society shared that belief. But he also knew what his friend was like with the ladies. Dangerous, because they were all so bloody attracted to the man.

He hadn't thought Holly had been taken in by Huntington's charms, but after overhearing them talk of secrets, he was suddenly doubting everything.

Particularly his own feelings for her.

Because damn it, he was starting to care for her, well beyond what he should or what was safe for him to. He'd never cared for a woman as much as he was coming to care for Holly and it scared the hell out of him.

"She has no interest in me," Huntington said, almost knowing what Michael had been thinking. "And goodness knows why she's so keen on you, but she is. So, after you've given her five minutes or so to calm down, stop being such a fool and go and apologize."

"Apologize?" Michael blinked. "For what?"

"Good lord, Blackthorn, you cannot be serious?" There was disbelief in Huntington's gaze. "Even *I* know one does not dictate to a woman without having to grovel in apology after."

"I can't imagine you ever apologizing."

Huntington grinned. "That's because I never earn their ire. Much more fun to pleasure them instead."

"Just you wait until you meet a lady who gets under your skin, as Holly does mine." Michael shook his head and exhaled harshly. "Then you'll be dictating left, right and center. Trust me."

The smile dropped from his face and though Huntington was looking at Michael, it felt like he was miles away, lost in memories. "Now that is a mistake, I will never make." Huntington blinked, almost as if he were pushing some bad memories aside and then returned his attention back to Michael. "But I am glad to see you've finally recognized you have feelings for the lady."

"Feelings?" Michael scoffed. "I don't have *feelings* for her. Well, except for annoyance. That, I regularly feel in her company." He didn't know why he didn't want to admit the truth to his friend, and why his cravat suddenly starting to feel far too tight. Of course, he cared about her. A part of him always had, not to mention he'd promised her brother he would. But it didn't go beyond caring. Did it?

"Well, I dare say that she's also feeling that particular emotion about you at the moment," Huntington said. "Annoyance, in spades."

"Oh, for goodness sakes," Michael exclaimed. "Surely she can't be that upset?"

"We are discussing the same woman who stormed out of here a short time ago, aren't we? The one who said she was done with you?" There was disbelief on his friend's face. "That woman is going to require groveling of the highest order to appease her ire."

Michael crossed his arms over his chest, much like Holly had done a short while ago. "I do not grovel." Though he had a sinking sensation that his words were mere bravado.

"Says the man who will be sleeping in a very cold bed until he does." Huntington walked over and patted him on the back. "Don't say I didn't warn you. I shall see you in London next week for my ball, I've decided not to stay after all."

Michael rubbed at the stubble on his cheek as he watched his friend walk away. *Feelings and groveling*? What on earth was happening to him? He felt like he was starting to fall down a rabbit hole and he didn't know how to stop himself. But Holly had always had an unsettling effect on him. Partly why he had stayed away from her, because he didn't trust his feelings when he was around her.

Huntington paused and looked back over his shoulder "Oh and Michael? Don't be a stubborn idiot and let her get away. Because if you do, I give you full warning, I shall pursue her." He winked at him, before striding through the doorway and out of sight.

When one had friends like that, who needed enemies, Michael thought darkly. As if he would let Huntington anywhere near Holly. Surely, she had only been venting when she'd broken things off with him? A part of him felt unusually panicked that perhaps she hadn't?

For a minute, he stood standing there ignoring the rather pointed looks from his peers, while he thought over what had just occurred and what Huntington had said. Unfortunately, it made sense as Holly had been furious. Which meant he probably would have to apologize, damn it. Especially as he knew he couldn't let her go. The very thought sent a shaft of fear all the way through him.

He'd have to tell her he was sorry and grovel in the process, he was sure of that. But damn it, he hated groveling. Perhaps if he spoke to her rationally, she would see his point of view and accept an apology, without any need to grovel.

With his mind made up, he left the veranda and strode down the hallway toward the front of the house, intent on getting to his room and the adjoining door to their bedrooms as soon as he could.

But the sound of a gunshot echoing further up the corridor brought him to an abrupt holt. Instinctively, Michael knew it involved Holly and that she was in danger. He broke out into a cold sweat.

Launching into a sprint, he ran down the hallway toward where the sound had come from.

Someone was screaming behind a closed door, up ahead on his left.

Racing over to the door, he rattled on the handle, but it was locked. Using his shoulder, he began ramming it against the door, desperate to get through to the other side. When the door barely budged, he took a step back and kicked at it with the sole of his boot. "Damn it! Open you stupid thing!" After two more attempts, the wood of the door frame split and the door flew inwards. It felt as if everything inside him froze upon the nightmare that greeted him.

Michael blinked, a tightness gripping his throat and anchoring his feet to the floor for a second, that seemed like an hour as his eyes stared at Holly, who was lying unnaturally still, in the middle of the floor, blood splattered over her dress and gushing from her head.

Blood roared to his head as he willed his feet to move. He rushed over to her, paying little attention to a man laying a few feet from her on the rug, with a hole in his chest and his eyes staring vacantly up to the ceiling, or of Lady Pembrook who was standing in the far corner of the room still screaming her head off.

"No, no, no..." Michael pleaded, skidding down onto his knees next to Holly. Dread knotted his stomach like a vice that wouldn't let go. "Please, be all right. Please, sweetheart, wake up." He wrenched his cravat from his neck and pressed it against the blood flowing from her forehead. "Holly wake up, sweetheart. Wake up!"

Images of Edward bleeding to death in front of his very eyes, swam across his vision. He'd been so helpless, pressing his cravat against the wound in his friend's chest while the white material quickly turned crimson as his friend's life blood soaked into it.

He'd lost his best-friend that day and he'd never fully recovered. But if he lost Holly... He couldn't lose her. He couldn't lose the only woman he'd ever truly cared about. His life simply wouldn't be worth living without Holly in it. He felt sick even thinking of such a possibility.

The woman might drive him mad with her bossy ways and how she would happily yell or chastise him, completely unafraid of him as no-one else was, but the idea of her not being around to do so, terrified him.

She'd always been on the periphery of his thoughts, ever since he could remember. Yet he'd always brushed such notions aside, reasoning she was Edward's sister and not to be trifled with. But somehow, she'd wormed her way into his heart.

He'd never loved anyone before, like he loved her.

The realization that he loved her completely, nearly bowled him over, but it suddenly wasn't as scary as he'd once imagined it to be. In fact, it was liberating. No longer was the fear of giving his heart to someone consuming him, because his heart had already quite happily given itself away without him even being aware of it.

But now she could leave him. Which he couldn't let that happen. He wouldn't!

Michael's eyes skimmed over her chest and he realized, in some surprise, that apart from the blood coming from the wound on her head, the other blood on her clothes didn't seem to be hers. Very gently he brushed his fingers over her chest and stomach, just to make sure. Definitely no wound, thank God.

Holly moaned softly. It was the sweetest sound he'd ever heard. Slowly she seemed to be starting to come to as her eyes blinked open.

Lady Pembrook continued wailing in the background.

"Damn it, that is enough!" he yelled across to the woman before turning his attention back to Holly. "It's all right, my darling. I'm here. You're safe now." He quickly looked back at Lady Pembrook who had stopped her crying. "What happened?"

The lady took a moment to compose herself. "She rushed the man and they struggled for a moment before the gun went off. Then Sir Reginald struck her on the temple with the butt of his pistol, before they both collapsed onto the floor."

Michael thought the man had looked vaguely familiar. Dark thoughts swirled in his head as he knew what Holly's uncle most likely would have been up to—forcing Holly to go with him, so she could marry his son. The bastard! Michael wasn't sorry about the man's death in the slightest. But he was concerned Holly had been cracked over the head with a pistol butt. She could be concussed, which was not a good thing.

Her eyes gradually focused on him and Michael found himself staring into the depths of a clear emerald ocean. Eyes that mesmerized him, and if he were being honest, always had. It was the most glorious sight he'd ever seen. "Oh, thank God," he prayed aloud, before bending down and kissing her softly on the cheek. "I was so worried," he whispered to her. "So, damned worried I didn't know what to do with myself. Are you all right?"

Slowly, she nodded. "My head is pounding though." Holly looked away, her gaze not meeting his. "What happened to my uncle?"

"He's dead I'm afraid," Michael said. "But that's not something for you to worry over. We need to get you seen by a doctor."

It was at that point, he heard the commotion as several people rushed into the room and some women's screams pierced the air. Swinging his head around, he saw Pembrook along with the butler and several guests standing at the threshold looking confused. "Damn it, get everyone out of here. You." He pointed to the Pembrook's butler. "Send someone to fetch a doctor immediately, and someone else to fetch a constable."

Pembrook still appeared confused, but his butler did as he had been instructed, hurrying out of the room.

"Perhaps a magistrate, would be more appropriate than merely a constable," Lady Pembrook spoke, having finally pulled herself together. "Mrs. Carlton was trying to steal from Lord Pembrook's safe I'm afraid, and Sir Reginald, rest his soul, tried to stop her, so she attacked and killed him. She will need to be arrested!"

There were several gasps from the guests that were still eagerly crowded around the doorway.

"That is a lie," Holly muttered, trying to push up from where she was laying. "Lady Pembrook was in league with my uncle, helping him to kidnap me, so I wouldn't find the evidence to prove she's been blackmailing people."

More gasps echoed from the door as Lady Pembrook hastily denied the allegation.

"Stay still, my darling, at least until the doctor sees you," Michael gently cautioned her.

"I'm fine," Holly insisted, carefully getting to her feet. "Besides, I don't want to be anywhere near him a moment longer." She glanced sideways at her uncle as she stood with Michael's assistance.

A second later though, she gripped hold of his arm and began to sway.

Scooping her up into his arms, Michael cradled her against his chest. "It's all right, my love, I have you." He strode to the door. "Move," he barked to the crowd, who all hastily began to scuttle away. "Pembrook, have this room closed, with a footman standing guard. The constable will want to inspect the body. As soon as the doctor gets here, send him to my room."

Pembrook nodded, as Michael began to carry Holly toward the staircase.

"But...but what about her?" Lady Pembrook screeched, pointing at Holly. "She's a murderer and a liar for suggesting I've had anything to do with blackmailing anybody!"

Michael paused in his stride and spun around, Holly still in his arms. "If I hear you've been spewing any such nonsense any further, you will rue the day. Do I make myself clear?"

Pembrook pulled his wife back toward him. "She won't say anything further, Blackthorn. I shall make certain of it."

"Be sure to, Pembrook. Or you will not like my reaction." Michael turned around and began to mount the staircase to the first floor, before striding down the hallway to his room. A minute later he safely deposited Holly on his bed and she lay back against the pillow with a slight whimper.

"Are you all right?" Michael asked pulling a chair over and sitting beside her.

She nodded. "I think so. It's just my head. It's pounding."

Leaning across, he peeled back his cravat that was still pressed against the wound on her forehead. Thankfully the bleeding was now simply a trickle. "Well you've definitely got a nice egg on your head, but the bleeding is easing up. Do you think you're up to telling me what happened?"

Succinctly, she told him what had occurred, but there was a distance in her voice and demeanor that troubled him. Perhaps she was still mad at him about earlier? But even that didn't feel right.

"So, Lady Pembrook is the one who has been dabbling in blackmail?" Michael murmured. "Makes sense why she was trying to paint you as guilty. We just have to find some proof she's guilty and then she'll be ruined."

"Consider her ruined." Holly pulled out a stack of papers from the pockets of her gown and spread them out onto the bed next to her. "I got in and out of her safe, retrieving all of these before they arrived."

"That's a lot of letters."

Holly nodded. "Goodness knows how many people she's blackmailed over the years or how many she intended to." She was silent for a minute before she spoke again. "She had a small dossier on you."

Michael raised a brow. "Me?" He wondered what sort of compromising information Lady Pembrook had gathered about him, for there had been a few situations over the years that could classify as compromising as he was neither a saint or a monk. Though there were none that he would ever be prepared to pay blackmail over. The very thought of Holly knowing about any of his liaisons or indiscretions over the years didn't sit well. Perhaps that's why she was acting so distant? "And what did it say?"

She licked her dry lips. "That you were the one responsible for Edward's death. That he died protecting you." Her eyes stayed staring into his. "Please, Michael, tell me it's not true."

Michael had never felt such a heaviness fill him. She knew. He could see the pain in her eyes, and with it the knowledge that she'd never forgive him. "It's true."

CHAPTER 14

HIS CONFIRMATION WAS DEVASTATING. All Holly wanted to do then and there was bury her head in the pillow next to her and cry. But she didn't. She had to maintain her composure or she'd fall to pieces. "So, you've lied to me ever since Edward's death."

Michael sat back on his haunches, his jaw clenched tightly, a look of unabashed guilt in his eyes. "I was wrong not to tell you the full truth. I know that, and I deeply regret doing so. But I never lied to you." He gingerly reached over and covered her hand with his. "I'm so sorry, Holly. I never meant to hurt you."

She snatched her hand away. "A lie by omission is still a lie." Holly felt like everything was shattering inside her. This man, who had slowly been weaving his way into her heart, had been deceiving her for years. "I think I finally deserve to know the *full truth* about how my brother died. Don't you?"

Taking in a somewhat ragged breath, Michael dragged a hand through his hair. "There hasn't been a day that's gone by since Edward died, that I haven't thought about him, or deeply regretted my actions."

"What happened?"

He pinched the bridge of his nose and sighed. "We'd just arrived at the Peninsula and the next morning we were due to march toward the battlefront. Several of us decided to go and have a drink at the local establishment, even though Edward cautioned us against doing so, but he came along, mostly to keep an eye on us I would say, as that was the sort of person he was. Everything was fine for a little while, we were all drinking and joking around, in a general attempt to forget what we were about to embark on in the morning." He took a deep breath and exhaled. "I started flirting with one of the women there, who had approached me, and when she suggested we go back to her lodgings I agreed.

"Edward tried to stop me of course, saying he was suspicious of the lady and her motives, warning me that it wasn't safe to go anywhere alone considering the hostilities in the region, particularly as I was rather foxed. But I of course ignored him. You see, before we left England I had probably one of the worst arguments I've ever had with my father. He was literally forbidding me to go to the Crimea, threatening to disown me if I dared to disobey him, so I told him to shove his title and I left. I think a part of me was hoping I would return in a coffin, just to stuff up the old man's carefully laid plans of succession. Isn't that ridiculous?" Michael laughed but there was no humor in the sound.

"That's why I also paid no heed to Edward's plea that night. I left the tavern with the woman and when we turned down the next laneway, two men came out of the shadows, clearly having been waiting for the woman to bring them someone to rob. Seeing them both holding daggers, I knew then I'd been a fool. A stupid one, who should have listened to Edward. But what was worse was that a part of me was almost baiting them to fight me, eager to take out my frustrations with my father on anyone, and I was just drunk enough to not care that they had weapons."

Michael paused for a moment and Holly could see that his fists were clenched tightly together, and he was holding himself very still.

"What happened then?" she asked.

He cleared his throat, and glanced away from her, his eyes staring vacantly out the window on the other side of the room, but she could see the sheen of tears in them. "Edward had followed us, and before I could even draw my own weapon, Edward jumped in front of me as one of the men lunged toward me, his dagger leading the way. Edward made this surprised sort of noise as the knife plunged into his chest and he fell back against me, while the two men fled."

With a jerk of his hand he wiped away the wetness from his eyes. "There was so much blood, everywhere. I pressed my cravat as hard as I could against the wound, but it turned red almost instantly. I screamed for help until my voice was hoarse. But by the time a doctor arrived, it was too late, Edward was gone."

Holly made no effort to brush away the tears that were now streaming down her face. The image of her brother like that was almost too much to bear.

"He was a hero," Michael continued. "Saving my worthless neck. I was angry at him for months after. I kept thinking if only he hadn't followed me, it would have been me that had been killed, not him. But then I realized I was actually furious at myself for not listening to him. For thinking I was invincible. Because if I hadn't been so stubborn, he wouldn't have died that night. So yes, I was responsible for his death. It is a burden I will forever carry with me and one I can never be absolved of."

"You should have told me sooner," Holly said, unable to look at him. There was a rage burning in her belly at the whole situation but also a deep sense of guilt. Because though a part of her was furious that Michael and his womanizing had created a situation that had caused the death of her brother, she was also consumed with guilt that a part of her was glad Michael had survived.

"I know," Michael agreed. "But I was scared that as soon as you learned the details of how I was responsible, you'd hate me and never forgive my actions. It was completely selfish of me, I know that and am so sorry for it. When I returned with his body for the funeral, I simply couldn't handle the thought of you all hating me, especially you. I didn't understand then why it troubled me so much if you despised me...but I understand now why it did."

She forced her eyes up to meet his and through her tears, she saw that he was struggling too. She wanted to hit and punch him for his role in it all and for not telling her. "And why is that? We've always bickered in the past that surely the thought of me hating you wouldn't have bothered you at all." She swung her legs to the side of the bed and sat up. "Do you know what I think, Michael Drake, I think you were a coward who didn't want to face the truth of the matter!" The anger she'd bottled up since her father and Edward's deaths, sprouted out of her like a fountain. "It was easier for you to say nothing and not implicate yourself at all, rather than tell the truth and ensure the blame was laid at your feet! I cannot believe that you let everyone think he died in a stupid drunken fight, alluding that he'd saved your life, but never going into the details to truly show that you are only alive today because of him!"

He slowly pushed back from his chair and stood. "I know I can't go back and change anything. But if I could, I would gladly give my life for his. Edward was always a better man than I and he would have lived a far better life than I have."

"I always used to chastise you for leading him astray!"

Holly cried. "You never listened. Neither of you did. If you had, Edward might still be alive. He's dead because of you!"

As soon as she said the words, she regretted them. But she was still too angry and hurt to try to take them back.

"I know. The knowledge is something I will always carry with me," Michael replied. "But before I go, I want you to know this." He walked behind his chair and placed his hands on the top frame of the seat. "The reason I didn't tell you then or before now, truly, was because the very idea of seeing the hate and repulsion in your eyes, the exact same expression that you're now looking at me with, terrified me. And the reason why it terrified me was because, I'm in love with you. A part of me has been for years, even though I refused to acknowledge it for a very long time."

Holly took in a shaky breath as his words hit her. He loved her? How dare he drop such a thunderbolt on her after admitting he'd been lying for years. "You bastard..." she ground out. Why would he tell her now that he loved her? And damn her traitorous heart for leaping at his words.

Guilt flooded her. She should be wanting his heart on a platter over his role in Edward's death, not feeling light headed with the thought of his love. What was wrong with her? She had to be the most disloyal sister on the planet to be in love with the man that was responsible for her brother's death.

Oh God. She loved him. How could she have let herself fall in love with him? She felt sick.

"I know I'm a bastard," he replied. "and I know I neither deserve or will get my love reciprocated, but I had to explain why I didn't tell you sooner."

A knock sounded on the door and both of them jolted, almost forgetting where they were.

Michael strode over to the door and let the doctor into the room, motioning toward Holly.

Holly wondered if the man could fix a broken heart.

"I will wait in the hall, until I know you're fine," Michael said, looking over at her. "Then I shall sort out the mess downstairs and the Pembrooks—trust me, they won't be bothering anyone again. I will organize for you to be taken safely back to London when you're fit to travel and then you can trust that I won't bother you again."

He bowed to her, and there was such a look of longing and wistfulness on his face, that Holly had to fight the urge to call him back. As desperately as a part of her was telling her to forgive him, she didn't think she could.

CHAPTER 15

IT HAD BEEN THREE-WEEKS, five days and nineteen hours since she'd last seen Michael when he'd left her with the doctor at the Pembrook's estate. Nearly four weeks of absolute misery.

Not a day had passed that Holly hadn't gone over their last conversation in her head, over and over again, until she didn't know if she'd imagined the part where he'd confessed his love. She was starting to think she probably had. After all, Michael was a rake of the first order, incapable of love, or so she'd thought.

How dare the man tell her he loved her after confessing that it was his actions that had gotten Edward killed? Why had he done such a thing?

"So, you're still moping about in here?" Violet's voice rang out from the doorway to Holly's study as she swept into the room. "Isn't it time to either get over it or go and tell him you love him too?"

Holly spun around to face her. "How can I love him; after what he did to Edward?" There was anger but also desperation in her voice.

Violet's expression softened as she came to stand in front of Holly and placed her hands on Holly's shoulders. "You're normally the smartest of us all, Holly, but in this situation you are being stupid."

Holly's jaw dropped open. "Excuse me?"

Her sister gave her a quick squeeze before her arms dropped down and she spun around to the window. She pulled open the drapes and Holly squinted as the blinding afternoon sun streamed into the previously darker room. "I said you are being stupid," Violet happily repeated.

"Do you not also blame him?" Holly asked her. "Edward was your brother too."

An expression of sorrow flickered over Violet's eyes. "It wasn't his fault, Holly, and I think you know that. Yes, if Michael had listened to Edward and not left with that woman, then Edward would probably not have died that night. But the fact is, that didn't happen. He chose to step in front of Michael and save his life that day, the foolish, brave brother that he was. Don't let his sacrifice in saving Michael, be for nothing. Don't ruin your chance of happiness by blaming Michael for the actions of another."

"But he should have said something sooner!" Holly declared. "He let us go on believing Edward's death was because of a tavern fight. He should have told us the full truth."

"But isn't that exactly what you're guilty of too?" Violet asked.

"What do you mean?"

"Well, you were pretending to be a widow and fooling everyone in Society for months."

"Yes, but I was only doing that to protect us." Holly slowly said. "I never actually said I was a widow. Michael simply believed what he'd heard from others."

"But you didn't tell him the truth about it, did you?" Her

sister pointed out. "You simply said nothing and let him believe what he'd heard. Exactly as we did with Edward's death. We simply accepted what others told us, never actually asking Michael for the truth, did we?"

"No, we didn't." Oh God, she hadn't.

"And what was it you told me you said to him?" Violet tapped a finger against her chin and pursed her lips, looking rather smug. "Oh yes, that's right, you said 'A lie by omission is still a lie'. That is what you said to him, isn't it?"

Holly felt like the biggest hypocrite imaginable. "I did say that...but he didn't correct us about how Edward actually died. By not saying anything he was protecting only himself. I at least was masquerading to protect you and Daphne."

"That may be true," Violet agreed. "But what was he protecting himself from?"

She thought back to that moment when he'd told her why, and it still made her heart beat fast. "He said he didn't say anything as he couldn't stand all of us hating him. Me especially."

"Exactly," Violet enthused, a smile lighting up her face. "He didn't tell you because he loved you, Holly. He was only trying to protect his heart, which is something I think we can all relate to. It's what you're doing now, after all."

"What do you mean?" Holly rounded on her sister.

Violet quirked her head to the side as she regarded her sister with somewhat disbelieving eyes. "I mean that the only reason you're so furious about his apparent deceit by omission is because you are afraid."

"Afraid?" Holly scoffed. "Afraid of what?"

"Of having your heart broken, sister." Violet sighed. "That is why you're doing all you can to keep telling yourself how mad you are with him."

"How can I love him, when Edward might have still been alive if it wasn't for him?" Holly felt her chest tighten painfully. "How can I be happy with him, knowing that Edward never had that same chance?"

Violet walked over to her and took her hands in her own. "Because Edward would want you to be happy. He would be thrilled to know that his best-friend and his sister were happy together. He would hate to know that he was the reason you were giving yourself, to lock your heart away and be miserable."

Slowly the truth of what Violet was saying, was starting to penetrate. Her sister was right. Edward had always been filled with happiness and laughter. He would hate to think he was the cause of why Holly was refusing to allow herself to be happy.

"I am a hypocrite, aren't I? Hiding behind my dead brother as an excuse to protect my heart."

"We all make mistakes," Violet conceded. "It is just lucky you have me here to see you don't continue to make them."

"I said some horrible things to him." Holly felt ill just thinking about it. "He'll never forgive me."

"Do you love him?"

Holly could only nod.

"Then you must tell him," Violet said. "You'll forever regret it, if you don't."

The thought of telling him, terrified her. "What if he doesn't love me anymore? What if he doesn't forgive me for the things I said?"

"I doubt that will be the case," Violet replied. "But you won't know until you muster the courage to find out. And if anyone can muster the courage, it's you, Holly. You are the most courageous woman I know."

Holly leaned over and hugged her sister tight. "Thank you, Violet. You're right, I shall have to go and face him." The prospect was daunting, but then the idea of not at least trying meant she would be allowing her fear to rule her. It was time to stop hiding from the possibility of being hurt.

She hadn't been able to control her father and brother dying and leaving them; a part of the reason why she'd been so afraid to give her heart to another man. But she wasn't going to lose Michael, without at least letting him know how she felt.

It was time to face Michael and tell him what was in her heart. And without further debate, she strode from her study and out into the entrance way. She swung her cloak onto her shoulders, before marching across to the front door and yanking it open.

She froze when she saw Michael standing on the front door stoop, his hand halted in midair.

CHAPTER 16

THEY BOTH STOOD THERE, staring at each other, for what felt like the longest time. Michael had never been more nervous, but he drunk in the sight of Holly, unable to look anywhere else but at her. He longed to sweep her up into his arms, but knew she'd probably start yelling at him to leave any moment.

"Before you say anything," he began, clearing his throat slightly in an effort to get rid of the sudden tightness. "I know you probably never want to see me again, but I couldn't not see you."

Holly remained standing there, the pulse at her neck beating rapidly, but thankfully there didn't seem to be anger in her gaze nor had she demanded he leave, which was possibly a good sign. Though he didn't want to get his hopes up too much.

Michael took in a deep breath. "I know I should have told you from the start what had happened with Edward, and I know I was a coward for not doing so. But I love you, Holly." He exhaled harshly, rushing on before she could stop him, "And if there's even the smallest of glimmers that you might be able to one day forgive me…then I will never give up hope that perhaps one day you might also agree to marry me, even if you don't love me…that doesn't matter to me. I love you and I want to spend a lifetime with you, looking after you and caring for you and your sisters, too. Please, Holly," he begged. "Please tell me if you think you could ever forgive me, even in the slightest? I know I don't deserve it, but I—"

She raised a finger up to his mouth, silencing him.

The very touch of her skin against his lips was a delicious torture. He'd missed her desperately and his body was craving hers. But he didn't dare touch her.

"I would never marry anyone that I didn't love with my whole heart," she said, and though the very sound of her voice sent a thrill through him, her words sent a shaft of agonizing despair straight to his heart.

Of course she couldn't love him. He'd been a fool to think otherwise. "I'm sorry to have bothered you," he muttered taking a heavy step backward and away from her. The loss of her finger against her lips sent a pang of anguish through him. "I won't do so again." He turned on his heel, but she grabbed his elbow and spun him around.

"Don't you dare go anywhere, Michael Drake!"

Confusion filled him. "I don't understand…"

"I said I won't marry anyone I do not love, didn't I?" She placed her hands on her hips and looked like she was impatiently awaiting an answer from him.

"Um, yes. You did say that." He scratched his head briefly. "But I'm not certain I understand?"

"It means that yes I will marry you."

"You will?" Michael felt his mouth hang open.

"Yes, I will." She smiled tremendously up at him. "I love you, you blockhead, so of course I will marry you."

"You do?" Slowly the confusion was giving way to joy as a big grin spread over his mouth.

She nodded. "I do."

He whooped and scooped her into his arms, swinging her around and around. She laughed aloud, and it was the sweetest sound Michael had heard.

Placing her back on her feet, he tilted her chin up toward him. "Are you sure? Even after what happened with Edward?"

Gently, she cupped his cheek with her palm. "His death wasn't your fault. Unfortunately, sometimes terrible things happen that we have no control over, and it can be easier blaming others. I'm sorry I blamed you. I know if the situation had been reversed, you wouldn't have hesitated to step in front of Edward, would you?"

"Of course not," Michael agreed. "If I could, I'd go back and give my life for his."

Holly brushed her fingers across his cheek. "I know you would. And I love you for it."

"You really love me?" A part of him couldn't quite believe she did. "You're too good to love me."

"I love you, Michael Drake," she assured him, leaning up and brushing her mouth against his. "I love you more than I ever thought it was possible to love anyone."

He bent his head down until his forehead touched her own and he stood there for a moment, just breathing in her smell. "God, I've missed you," he confessed. "And I love you, Holly Jenkins. I will love you for the rest of my life."

"As will I, you," Holly whispered.

Reluctantly, he pulled away from her and looked her steadily in the eyes. "Will you marry me, my mistletoe mistress? Will you make me the most ecstatic of blockheads in the world?"

A great burst of laughter flew out of her mouth. "Oh, my darling blockhead, yes I will marry you."

To know that Holly was going to be his wife, filled him

with a sense of deep contentment and joy. For the first time in his life, he was truly happy.

Softly, his lips descended down onto her own and he kissed her with all of the love he felt. A kiss that was breathtaking in its sweet intensity. A kiss that heralded the start of their life together.

And with Holly in his arms, he was finally home.

EPILOGUE

ONE YEAR later

"You wouldn't believe it," Holly declared, waltzing into his study and emphatically waving a letter about in her hand. "The Devil Duke has finally returned to England and is looking for a wife!"

Michael glanced up from his ledger and raised a brow. "You are correct. I don't believe it." He leaned back in his chair, delighting in watching his wife's animated face as she strode over toward him. They'd been married for just over six months and he was more in love with her than he'd ever been.

"Well it is true," Holly said, reaching his side and bending down to press her lips against his in a leisurely kiss. Slowly she pulled back from him and grinned. "I have it on the best of authorities. Devlin Markham, the Duke of Huntington is looking for a wife."

"Who is your source? Lady Winthrup?"

Holly nodded as she perched her delightful derriere on the edge of his desk. "Mable Winthrup is the best source of information in all of London."

"The best gossip, don't you mean?" Michael teased her.

"That too." Holly grinned. "But she's always been correct. She knew all about your wager, didn't she now?"

He reached out and encircled her waist, before pulling her fully onto his lap. "She did. Though I highly doubt she's correct about Devlin looking for a wife. The man has far more misgivings about the institution of love and marriage, then I ever did. And that is saying something."

"But just look how happy you are now," Holly pertly reminded him. "I think marriage would be wonderful for him. He's very lonely."

Michael laughed. "Please! The man is never in want of female company."

Holly raised her chin. "That does not mean he's not lonely."

"True," Michael conceded, resting his head against her cheek and breathing in the delicious scent of rosewater on his wife's neck. Before Holly, he hadn't realized how desperately lonely he'd been. "Goodness, you smell delicious. I don't think I can ever get enough of you." He gently started to rein kisses across the column of her throat.

She sighed in pleasure and pressed herself even closer to him. "You'll also be interested to know," she said, her voice getting rather breathless as it always did when she was starting to become aroused. "Lord and Lady Pembrook have fled to the continent."

"Have they?" He continued feathering kisses along her jawline. "That's nice to know."

"You don't sound very interested or surprised." She pulled back from him, suspicion in her emerald eyes.

"I'm a bit more preoccupied with my gorgeous wife, to be honest." Michael tried to edge his lips closer to her, but she pressed her hand up against his chest.

"You didn't happen to have anything to do with them fleeing, did you?"

"Not really." Michael began to trail his fingers up along the sides of her waist, until he was softly cupping her breasts. Satisfaction filled him when her gaze deepened with passion. "The whispers of Lady Pembrook blackmailing others had well and truly caught momentum long before now. I'm only surprised they didn't flee sooner."

"I suppose so."

"Now, where was I?" His lips caught hers, softly teasing them apart and kissing her until she was moaning, his hands continuing to gently squeeze her breasts.

"Wait," she panted, pulling back from him. "I have one more bit of news."

"Can't it wait?" he asked. "There are other things I'd rather focus my complete attention upon."

She laughed but refused to allow his lips to capture hers again. "I think you'll be particularly interested in this bit of news."

"Let me guess," his whispered against her ear. "It has to do with Violet and St. Giles, and the fact they seem to be spending a great deal of time together at balls and the like."

"What?" Holly screeched. "Violet and St. Giles, spending time together? But they can't stand one another."

Michael sighed and pulled his lips back from the delectable skin of his wife's neck. "I thought you knew?"

"Knew what?" Her eyes were dark, but unfortunately not with passion any longer. "If that bounder is daring to seduce my sister, why that is... well it's not acceptable. You must put a stop to it, Michael! It's bad enough that Daphne is already considered a diamond of the first water and we must put up with all her callers, but Violet and St. Giles? No. My sister surely isn't interested in that rake. You must talk to him and warn him away."

"Me?" The very thought of interfering in his sister-in-law and friend's business was not a pleasant one. "Violet can handle herself with St. Giles. In fact, I think he's rather smitten with her, not that he'd ever admit it."

"Please!" Holly scoffed, sarcasm dripping from her voice. "That man is smitten with half the women in London. He's a rake through and through, who gets hives when someone simply mentions the word marriage in his presence."

Michael chuckled, for her description was apt. "But rakes can be reformed, my love." He slowly reached his hands around his wife's waist and rubbed her back. "Am I not the perfect example of that?"

"Yes, you are," she relented, relaxing her back into his hands. "Though I hate the thought of Violet getting her heart broken."

"Your sister will run rings around St. Giles, my love. Trust me." Michael nuzzled the pulse at her throat with his lips. "Now what else did you want to tell me before I become entirely distracted?"

"Oh, yes." Holly's whole demeanor shifted in an instant, almost as if she was bracing herself. "I went and saw Doctor McGuiness today, who was recommended to me by Lady Winthrup—"

"Doctor McGuiness?" Michael's hand stilled and he pulled back to stare at Holly. "Isn't he that Scottish doctor that all the ladies swoon over?"

Holly shrugged. "Yes, that's him. He's considered rather handsome actually, though of course he's not as handsome as you, my love," she was quick to assure him.

Michael didn't like it one bit. "Well what the devil do you need to see a doctor about anyway? I thought you'd recovered from that bout of indigestion the other day?"

"Turns out it's slightly more serious than we first thought and will probably take longer to resolve."

His heart slammed in his chest as fear coiled through him with the thought that something was wrong with Holly. "What do you mean?" A myriad of possibilities roared through his head. Each one worse than the last.

"Well my love…" Holly squared her shoulders and took in a deep breath.

Panic gripped him when he saw the sheen of tears swimming in her eyes. "Oh God, what is it?"

"I'm pregnant…" Her voice trailed off and Michael could only blink.

"Pregnant?"

She nodded and the tears that had been threatening, spilled over onto her cheeks as a huge smile spread across her lips. "Yes." She took his hand in hers and brought it down to rest on her belly. "We're having a baby."

He glanced down to where his hand lay upon the smooth blue velvet of her dress. Never had he been so lost for words before. He cleared his throat and looked up at Holly. She was pregnant with his child?

The most overwhelming sense of wonder and joy filled him, and for a minute he couldn't move. He was going to be a father. The thought was both terrifying and thrilling.

She bit her bottom lip. "Are you pleased?"

"Pleased? I'm beyond pleased, my love. I'm ecstatic." He cupped her face with his hands and brushed his thumbs across her cheeks. "You have made me and continue to make me the happiest of men, my darling Holly." He softly pressed his lips against hers with such tenderness and love. "Though I will admit, the idea of being a father is somewhat frightening, particularly after the example my own father has set."

"He's rather critical of you," Holly agreed. "Though he has gotten somewhat better since we've been married."

It was true, his father had always been so exacting, that

nothing Michael did was ever good enough. Until he'd married Holly. His father adored Holly and finally thought Michael had done the family proud. Which had been a shock to Michael initially as he'd assumed that because Holly was not an earl or duke's daughter, that his father would have considered her unacceptable to marry his son.

But as soon as the man had met Holly, she'd bowled the curmudgeon over. Of course, Michael should have known she would. Everyone who met Holly adored her. She was just so lovable that even now he couldn't believe it had taken him this long to realize how much he loved her. "He's gotten better because he finally agrees with me on something."

"And what is that?"

"That I made the best decision of my life when I fell in love with you."

"As did I, when I agreed to marry you," Holly countered as she kissed him back. "You will make a wonderful father, Michael. You are so kind and caring. The best person I know."

"You're an optimist my love." Michael smiled. "But I hope you're right." He rubbed his hand across her belly again, marveling that his baby was growing inside her. "I shall try to be the very best father and I'm going to love our child fiercely."

"I know you will, my love."

He rested his forehead against her own and breathed in deeply. "Damn I love you Holly, more than I ever thought I could love someone. The strength of my feelings are sometimes overwhelming."

"Oh, Michael, I love you so very much too."

"If it's a boy, what do you think about naming him, Edward?"

Her eyes filled with further tears, but there was such

happiness sparkling in their depths that it filled his heart with joy.

"I think that would be perfect," she whispered, before leaning over and kissing him with such breathtaking softness, that it stole his breath away.

In that moment, he felt complete. And with Holly by his side, life would be a journey he would cherish always.

READ AN EXCERPT OF THE
DEVILISH DUKE

BY MADDISON MICHAELS

London, 1855

The night was turning into an utter disaster.

Lady Sophie Wolcott strode down the gas-lit path edging the gardens of the Duke of Huntington's palatial townhouse, the soft strains of music emanating from the nearby ballroom a constant reminder that this particular ball was not going as expected.

Instead of dancing with the man of her dreams, she was forced to spy upon him. Really, what else could she do after he disappeared into the library with another woman?

And the library was on the second floor. That could pose a problem.

Disregarding her new ball gown snagging on the twigs and branches lining the path, Sophie spotted an old oak tree directly below the library window. That would do.

Her mind set, she trudged over to the stone bench positioned next to the trunk. She glanced in both directions...not a soul around. Luckily, most of the guests were occupied by the notorious Duke of Huntington's lavish affair—at least she prayed they were.

Steeling her resolve before all of the ways in which her plan could go horribly wrong overcame her, she deftly lifted the skirts of her gown and untied the string of her crinoline, letting it drop to the ground. She kicked it under the bench and gathered the petticoats and material of her dress in her hands.

Before she could change her mind, she stepped up onto the bench and grabbed hold of the branch hanging above with her free hand. Putting her foot into the small groove of the trunk, she rather awkwardly swung herself up until she was comfortably straddling the branch. Thankfully, she had not lost her knack for climbing trees, though it certainly hadn't been as cumbersome when she had been a girl wearing a pinafore instead of a ball gown.

She glanced around the gardens. Still deserted. Not that anyone would be all that surprised to find her up a tree, given her reputation as a bluestocking and a bit of an eccentric. Though she'd prefer not to give the gossips any further morsels for their ravenous tongues, if she could avoid it.

"You can do this, Sophie," she murmured to herself, forcing her eyes forward instead of straying down to the shrubs below. "It's not that high." She could hear the lack of conviction in her own words, but she was on a mission and would not be deterred. Deftly, she pressed her body flat onto the bark and began carefully edging her way across to the window until she could see through the glass.

She pushed away some wayward golden curls from her forehead and looked into the room until she saw Richard, the Earl of Abelard, standing near the hearth. He was so handsome with his light brown hair and those vivid green eyes. He'd always struck her as heaven sent, looking rather like an angel.

An angel she'd always thought she was destined to marry.

A sigh escaped her lips. He had been ever so kind to her at her mother's funeral all those years ago, when she was only eight, that she had known since then that he would eventually make her the perfect husband. He liked books, he always asked about her charity work at the orphanage and listened attentively when she talked, and...those eyes.

Now all she had to do was convince *him* of that, too. A rather difficult endeavor, considering that for the past fifteen years, he'd only seen her as his younger sister's best friend.

Sophie scowled when she saw Miss Grace Davies with him—a woman all of the gossiping old biddies of the Ton claimed had captured his heart. The old biddies had to be wrong. The Earl was far too sensible to be taken in by such a superficial female. Why, the only time Sophie had ever conversed with Miss Davies, the woman had spent the entire conversation discussing her latest reticule and pointing out all of the bachelors vying for her attention.

Gripping the branch harder, she leaned slightly forward when he got down on one knee and pulled out a small box from his pocket. Surely he was not proposing? No. Fate could not be so cruel.

But evidently it was.

Sophie gasped in stunned horror as Richard placed the ring onto the woman's finger before standing and softly kissing her.

That hurt. Quite badly.

She could only gape as they both gently parted and smiled at one another before walking to the door and leaving the room. As the door closed behind them, Sophie could literally feel her dreams crumbling into a pile of dust.

She laid her cheek against the rough bark of the branch and let herself dangle in misery. Perhaps she would join a nunnery? Though waking up at dawn and practicing devout obedience were not duties she was all that keen to embrace.

No, it would be best she remain a dedicated scholar, helping the children at the orphanage learn to read and write, as her mother had done before her. After all, keeping her mother's vision for Grey Street Orphanage alive was what was important and what Sophie had to focus on. And if she could not marry the man she'd had her heart set on, since childhood, she would prefer to not marry any man.

The sound of a wholly different man and woman's laughter flittering across the gentle night breeze interrupted her thoughts. Twisting her head, she peered out into the darkness, but the dim light from the gas lamps cast a soft glow on the path, and she could only see vague shadows in the distance. But those shadows were clearly heading in her direction and getting closer.

She sighed. Fate was surely having a grand old time at her expense. Here she was up an oak tree, her longtime beloved engaged to another, and a couple had obviously decided to cavort with each other in the gardens before she could get down.

Edging her body backward, she gritted her teeth at the coarse bark grating roughly under her gloves. She stopped and gripped the branch hard as it began to wobble. Perhaps her wretched luck this evening would change, and the couple would keep walking by without even realizing she was above them.

The couple strolled closer, murmuring in the darkness. She held her breath, disbelieving as the man sat down on the stone bench below. She could see them quite clearly now, in the circle of light from a nearby lamp, and prayed that she was not equally visible to them.

What more could go wrong?

Instead of sitting down next to the gentleman, the lady sat upon his lap.

She felt her jaw drop open. That was definitely not proper behavior.

She blinked when the man claimed the woman's mouth in what was the most carnal kiss Sophie had ever witnessed. A kiss at complete odds with the chaste one Richard had bestowed on Miss Davies but a moment ago.

Sophie started to feel uncomfortably hot and bothered as an unfamiliar warmth curled in her belly.

"Devlin," the woman moaned, "we must hurry before my husband realizes I am gone."

A small gasp of surprise escaped Sophie's lips, and she immediately held her breath, hoping they hadn't heard her. Devlin, as in the *Duke of Huntington?* And he had a married lady sitting astride him? Did the man have no morals whatsoever?

Obviously, the rumors circulating about him being an out and out rake were indeed true. No wonder everyone called him the Devil Duke, if this was the sort of shenanigans he took part in.

Her moral outrage aside, she couldn't help but admire the way the light hit the hard angles of his face, the full mouth that he obviously used to his advantage in more ways than one. She craned her neck to get a better look.

Her body began to slip.

She hugged the branch as hard as she could, but her satin gloves were slowly losing their grip, and she began tilting precariously to the side. "Oh dear!" she yelped, a second before gravity took over, and she tumbled from the branch.

"What the hell..." the Duke growled as Sophie landed in the shrubbery below.

She lay there, too dazed to feel embarrassed, her head thrown back and her back arched across a particularly uncomfortable azalea. Then slowly, she blinked. Someone's feet began crunching through the knee-high plants, so she pulled herself out of her stupor and turned toward the noise. She saw some black boots, followed by a pair of perfectly tailored trousers, covering some very long and muscular legs.

Of course he would have excellent legs as well...

"Are you hurt?" the Duke asked, crouching down.

Considering his question, she adopted what she hoped was a blasé expression, as if ladies tumbled out of trees on a regular basis. It did not feel as if anything was broken. "No, just dazed, I think..."

She rolled into a slightly more dignified position and lifted a hand to rub her temple, finding her gaze held captive by the most wickedly handsome man she'd ever seen. From this angle, all of the shadows were cast from his face. Gleaming white teeth flashed sinfully against bronzed skin, and dark stubble covered his jawline in a manner that was frowned upon by the majority of Society but gave him an air of dashing danger.

And from the highly thorough onceover he was giving her, she could tell the man had earned every bit of his notorious reputation as a rake.

"Well, no wonder. What the devil were you doing up a tree?" he asked.

"Surely that is obvious," the lady screeched as she stood by the edge of the garden bed, some wayward flaming red curls, which had escaped her chignon, bobbing wildly around her. "She is spying on us, at the behest of my husband no doubt."

"Felicity, enough with the theatrics."

"She was spying on us, I tell you," Felicity insisted.

"I was not." Sophie struggled to sit up, rolling in what she hoped was at least a somewhat graceful manner onto the soft green plants surrounding the azalea.

"Of course you were," Felicity continued, circling Sophie like a cat about to pounce. "I would not be surprised—"

"Enough!" the Duke commanded, his tone brooking no argument. He looked down at Sophie. "Stay still while I check if you have any broken bones."

"No, that would be completely inappropriate!" Sophie knocked his hands away from near her ankles. "Besides, I am fine." Pushing her body up, she felt a sharp pain slice up the small of her back, and she winced.

"Perhaps now you will stay still?" the Duke asked as he placed his hands upon her shoulders and held her in place. "It may be inappropriate, but it is necessary. I promise not to hurt you, all right?"

Finding her gaze trapped by his ridiculously blue eyes, she saw the truth mirrored back in them. Slowly, she nodded.

"For goodness sakes, Devlin," Felicity rasped, "the girl said she is fine. We must leave before we are discovered." She picked up the skirts of her ruby dress, which, even though it covered her from shoulder to ankle, still had an air of scandal about it.

"Stop being so heartless for once in your life, Felicity," the Duke admonished as he quickly patted his hands over the material of Sophie's deep blue gown, checking for any injuries to her legs. Deep down, she knew she should swat him away, but she just sat, mesmerized by the conversation and by his touch.

Felicity put her hands on her hips. "You, of all people, call me heartless? How can you speak—"

"If you are going to be of no assistance," Devlin interrupted, "leave."

The other woman bared her teeth. "Well, if you think you shall ever have another opportunity with me, you are highly mistaken." She whirled around toward the direction of the ballroom.

"A tragedy to be sure, but Felicity"—the Duke's voice

became deadly soft—"this incident tonight is not to be discussed with anyone, or I shall call your husband's markers in. Do I make myself clear?"

Felicity slowly swiveled around and faced him. It appeared the lady's complexion had become even paler. "I assure you that no matter how much of a cad you may be, it would be beneath me to gossip about us or some idiotic girl who fell out of a tree."

Sophie opened her mouth to reply but then closed it again. Truthfully, her behavior could arguably be called idiotic. What had she been thinking? Actually, that was the problem. She hadn't been thinking at all. It was her heart that had led her astray. Well, no more.

"Good. See that it remains so," Huntington said.

Felicity's eyes glittered with malice before she turned and strode off down the path.

"Do not pay her any mind," the Duke said, continuing to gently examine Sophie's legs with his hands. "She will not disobey me."

A small shiver ran through her from his touch. She did her best to mentally brush it aside. "I shall not worry overly," she muttered. "My future plans are already ruined. Though I do suppose my aunt would care. If she ever found out, I am certain she would have a permanent fit of the vapors. And then my life would *truly* be a nightmare."

He ignored her dramatics completely. "What is your name?"

She sighed, supposing she would have to tell him. "Lady Sophie Wolcott, Your Grace."

"Ah, Lady Sophie, and it appears as though you know who I am. Perhaps then you should call me Devlin."

The man's lack of proprietary knew no bounds. Though she couldn't say she was particularly surprised. He had obviously earned his reputation. If he thought issuing such an untoward invitation would have any effect on her, he was sorely mistaken. "That would be highly improper," she said. "As well you know, *Your Grace.*"

"Your decision," he said, sitting back on his haunches. "Now it seems as though nothing is broken."

"Apart from my heart," she mumbled.

"A useless muscle." His startling blue eyes bored into her own. "However, you did have a rather decent fall. How do you feel?"

"Sore and somewhat mortified. However, I shall recover." She pushed Abelard and his fiancée firmly out of her mind before she could consider whether she'd ever recover from the scene she'd recently witnessed. Carefully, she started to rise. The duke offered her his hands, and when she took them, he pulled her to her feet.

"So you think yourself in love then?"

"That is none of your concern." A flutter of awareness shot down to her toes. His hands were strong. *My goodness.* What on earth was wrong with her? The fall had to have unsettled her more than she realized to make her react in such a manner from his touch.

When she was steady on her feet, he released her. "Love is a wasted emotion that only brings with it heartache and loneliness. It is an utter waste of time to dwell on. The sooner you realize that, the better you shall be."

"You have a very cynical attitude about the matter." She dusted her palms off and focused on calming her suddenly erratic heartbeat. Instinctively, she knew this was a man who would take advantage of any sign of weakness, much like a predator.

"Perhaps." He agreed, though he sounded unfazed by the notion. "But I rather think of it as being pragmatic. I myself have never been caught falling out of a tree."

Folding her arms across her chest, she narrowed her eyes.

"I shall have you know that my future happiness was torn apart tonight, and only the direst of circumstances compelled me to climb a tree!" Though, oddly enough, she wasn't feeling nearly as heartbroken as she would have expected to. It seemed her verbal sparring with the Devil Duke was enough to cheer her spirits considerably.

The duke said nothing; he merely continued to watch her. Sophie had the bizarre sensation that he was cataloguing her soul. She shivered in spite of herself.

"Are you cold?" he enquired, scanning her wrists as if to check for goosebumps.

"No," she was quick to reply. For some strange reason, even though she was standing in the shrubs outside in the middle of the night and having a conversation with the Devil Duke, she felt oddly safe.

Although, if anyone happened upon them, she was sure to be ruined. Not that she was particularly worried over such an occurrence; she had no intention of marrying now, after all, but her aunt would be devastated.

"Come, let us get you out of the garden," his deep voice drawled. "Then you can amuse me with your explanation about what you were doing up one of my trees." He strode back through the shrubs toward the path.

She rather thought his words sounded like an imperial command. She brushed off the small bits of bark and twigs clinging to her gown and then took a step forward. Blast! Looking down, she saw the hem of her dress was happily entangled in the shrubs. "Darn!" Her luck just kept getting worse and worse.

"First, you fall from a tree, and now you are cursing," he murmured. "I did not think young ladies were taught such interesting etiquette."

She felt like displaying to him just what sort of unusual etiquette she'd been taught as she tugged harder on her gown. It still refused to budge. She couldn't believe she was going to have to ask this bounder for his help. How mortifying. "My dress appears to be caught."

"Stuck, are you?"

"How very astute." She smiled through gritted teeth. "Now would you please be so kind as to help me?"

"I thought I had already done so. What are you willing to offer for my further assistance?"

Sophie paused, wholly unsure of the Duke's intentions. "What do you mean?"

He smiled, though it did not reach his eyes. "I have already lost Lady Astley's company tonight to assist you. Why should I help you once again without suitable reward for my services?"

Was he really suggesting what she thought he was? Surely not. And if he was, she certainly wouldn't give him the satisfaction of revealing her awareness to what he was alluding to. "Because it is the right thing to do, of course."

His eyes held hers, and she suddenly felt pinned down by his intense blue gaze. Even in the semi-darkness, they were striking. Then, he ruefully chuckled, and the trance was broken. "Doing the right thing. How novel." A grin danced across his insanely sensual lips. Walking back through the shrubs, he reached around her and pulled on her dress. "You have snagged yourself well."

"Trust me, I shall not be wearing one of these silly lace gowns again." She watched as he bent down toward his boots. "What are you doing?"

"Helping you." He pulled out a dagger from his boot.

Her eyes widened as the lamp light glinted off the sharp steel of the most vicious-looking blade she had ever seen. And he was carrying it around in his boot? "No. You are not to use that anywhere near me."

"I am afraid I must, my lady." He had an air of amusement about him that made her feel decidedly annoyed.

"And I am afraid you must not." *Goodness*, his reputation for danger was clearly warranted. No other gentleman she knew would have a need, let alone dare, to carry around a knife on his person.

"Very well." He re-sheathed his dagger. "I shall simply have to unlace your dress and then you can slip free of it." He looked rather happy at the prospect.

"Excuse me?" Sophie was dumbfounded. The man's suggestion was outrageous. "I am not taking my dress off in front of you! Have you lost your mind entirely?"

"No." He stopped for a moment, however, as if to consider whether that actually was the case. "But either the gown comes off, or I use the knife to cut it free. They are the only two options available. I'd prefer the first, obviously." The cad winked at her.

"The knife shall be perfectly fine."

Huntington laughed and retrieved his dagger. "I rather thought it would." He bent down, and with a quick flick of his wrist, he cut the trapped piece of lace free from the rest of her skirt. "There you are."

Never one to worry overly much about her clothing, she shook out her dress and followed him through the shrubs to the path.

"I must say that your gown is looking oddly deflated. I think I may have seen the edge of your crinoline peeking out from under the stone bench." His lips twitched at the corner.

Rushing over to the bench, she leaned down and picked the hoop up.

"Do you intend on putting it back on?" he drawled.

"Certainly not with you here, Your Grace." Goodness, the man was incorrigible!

He grinned. "I can look away if you prefer, or assist? I

must say, though, that my experience with such things relates more to getting the contraption off."

"Why does that not surprise me at all?" Sophie tried to banish the sudden image of him standing behind her, his breath whispering across her ear as his fingers brushed across her waist while he laced it up.

"But you are an odd duck, are you not?" He leaned against a lamppost, as if making himself comfortable so he could take in the spectacle that she was about to create. "Most ladies would not dare to be caught without their crinoline safely shaping their dresses."

She put her free hand on her hip. The fabric of her gown concealed all it covered, crinoline or no, but she still felt exposed under his gaze. "I could not very well climb a tree with it on, now could I?"

"True," he said, "it would have made the endeavor practically impossible. Which does beg the question, what were you doing up a tree in the first place?"

"I was... Actually, that is not your concern." She placed the crinoline on the bench just so she could cross her hands forbiddingly over her chest. "Besides, you should be ashamed of yourself, sir, carrying on with a married lady. Falling from the tree when I did was probably divine intervention."

His laughter once again echoed through the night. "I am sure tonight has been highly instructive for you."

She had the grace to blush as the memories of what he had recently been doing not five minutes before assailed her.

"From the heat stealing across your cheeks, Lady Sophie, I shall assume it was."

The urge to throw something at his arrogant smirk nearly overwhelmed her. She had half a mind not to respond, though that would be childish. "Watching you and your mistress is not something I would ever care to see again, Your Grace."

His lips twitched. "So you think Lady Astley is my mistress?"

"The fact that she was straddling your lap and moaning your name aloud might have given me an inkling," she scoffed. "I see that the gossip concerning you has turned out to be remarkably correct. *You*, sir, *are* an out and out libertine."

"I do try," he said, his face completely serious. "I must say that the gossip circulating about yourself has also proved extremely accurate."

"Gossip?" Who was making up stories about her? "There is no gossip about me. Is there?"

"Eccentricity is always gossiped about in the Ton." He grinned. "Though, apart from your unusual charity work at orphanages, I must say that your little midnight rendezvous are not common knowledge."

"Midnight rendezvous... Why, it was nothing of the sort." Trust a libertine such as he to assume such a thing, when it could not be further from the truth. Involuntarily, she looked up at the library window.

Huntington's eyes followed. "My, my... You are a little spy. Though I assume you got slightly more of a show than you had bargained for when Lady Astley and I interrupted."

"I shall have you know, Your Grace, that I was not spying upon your dalliance. Rather, I was looking for my beloved." It felt good to tell him her heart belonged to another. All the better to keep up the pretense that his nearness had no effect on her.

"Up a tree?" He chuckled. "This night continues to get more amusing by the moment. But tell me, are you not a tad young to have a beloved?"

"I'm not that young. Regardless, love cares naught for age; it is pure," she insisted. "Though after what I have witnessed this evening, I was most recently considering joining a convent."

His rich laughter again ricocheted through the night. "Made that much of an impression on you, did I?"

She lifted her chin high into the air. "Do not give yourself unwarranted praise, *Your Grace.*"

"It is never unwarranted. Of that you can be sure." There was a heated and determined promise in his gaze that sent a fluttering through her belly, unsettling her greatly.

That he could have such an effect on her already was particularly disturbing. Taking in a deep breath, she continued on. "Truth be told, it was the very sight of the man of my dreams, a most wonderful earl, embracing his new fiancée that put the thought in my head."

"You do not mean that nauseating do-gooder, the Earl of Abelard, do you?"

"How dare you call him that? He is the most honest, most selfless, most wonderful man in all of England." Apart from the minor issue of his proposing to the wrong woman, of course.

"Yes, well...England is rather small." Huntington once again sounded bored as he pulled a cheroot from his pocket and examined it, as if weighing whether it would be worth smoking in front of a lady.

"The world then!" she said. "The Earl is infinitely more of a gentleman than you, and he would never kiss a married woman such as you did."

"True. I doubt he has the aptitude for it."

"Stop mocking him."

The man simply grinned. "But you take the bait so well. Now surely your chaperone must be frantic as to your whereabouts by this stage?"

Sophie cringed slightly as a flutter of guilt assailed her. "Actually, I think my aunt Mabel may be under the mistaken impression that I had a headache and borrowed the carriage to go home."

"An impression given to her by you, no doubt?"

Reluctantly, she bobbed her head in agreement.

"I pity the poor sap that gets saddled with you." He sighed. "Very well, I shall send my carriage around to take you home to bed. There you can dream of your beloved and of his new fiancée's early demise."

"That is a terrible thing to suggest." Sophie smoothed down the skirts of her gown. "No one could be horrid enough to wish someone dead."

Huntington's expression flattened. "In that, my dear lady, you are wrong. Very wrong."

She shivered; his eyes were now a wintry blue, all humor having fled. "Why do you say that?"

His bleak look seemed to vanish, only to be replaced by an enigmatic lack of expression. "Do you know the grand occasion this ball is in honor of?"

"I believe it is being held in your late grandfather's honor," she whispered.

"Yes, it is. It's a celebration, you see. Though not to celebrate his life, Lady Sophie, but rather to celebrate his death."

"His death?" she asked. Surely, the Duke didn't mean he had wanted his grandfather to die?

"Indeed," he confirmed. "As far as I'm concerned, the old codger can burn in hell."

Goodness. It seemed there was no end to the man's penchant for being shocking. "But saying such a thing is... blasphemous."

The corners of his mouth stretched into a tight smile as he brought the cheroot to his lips, and then he clamped down on it with his teeth so he could light it. The end of the cigar glowed red in the lamplight, and smoke curled around his head. "Hadn't you heard, my dear? I am the Devil Duke. My very existence is blasphemous. Now run along, or else I will assume you wish me to show you just how much of a devil I can be."

The expression on his face was dark and heated. And suddenly, Sophie felt alarmed— not of him, but rather of her own response. Because rather than scare her, as she was sure had been his intention, his words had instead inflamed her body, sending a thrum of desire through her.

Then just as suddenly, the thought that she could actually be attracted to a rake felt like someone had thrown a bucket of ice over her head. She would not allow a man of his ilk to charm and beguile her, as her mother had allowed Sophie's father to. She'd vowed that a long time ago, and not even the Devil Duke, with his sinfully handsome face and equally seductive body, would sway her.

She spun around and fled into the night.

~

**To purchase THE DEVILISH DUKE,
winner of the 2019 Australian RWA Historical Romance
Book of the Year,
visit:
https://books2read.com/TheDevilishDuke**

ACKNOWLEDGMENTS

A huge thanks to fellow historical romance author Emmanuelle de Maupassant - who is so generous and supportive! She is such a fabulous example of an author who happily helps others and is an absolute credit to the profession! Em was the one who organized the wedding boxed set 'Once Upon A Christmas Wedding', that this novella was originally part of. It was because of this boxed set that I decided to give novella writing a go, and I'm so glad I did as I had such fun writing Michael and Holly's story! And I do foresee writing many more novellas (Holly's sisters do need their own story told, after all!). So a BIG thank you, Em (especially for all of your patience with my questions)!

ABOUT THE AUTHOR

Indoctrinated into a world of dashing rogues and feisty heroines when she was a teenager, Maddison Michaels is a bestselling, award-winning Australian romance author, who loves to write sexy history with a dash of mystery! Her debut novel, THE DEVILISH DUKE, won the 2019 Romance Writers of Australia Historical Romance Book of the year. Maddison lives in Sydney with her gorgeous hubby and daughter, and always starts her day with a cup of liquid gold... coffee (just quietly, she's addicted to the stuff)!

For more books and updates visit:
www.maddisonmichaels.com

www.ingramcontent.com/pod-product-compliance
Lightning Source LLC
Chambersburg PA
CBHW030431120726
47903CB00003B/917